*Radiance*

# Radiance

## TEN STORIES

*Winner of the Sandstone Prize in Short Fiction*

John J. Clayton

OHIO STATE UNIVERSITY PRESS

COLUMBUS

**Library of Congress Cataloging-in-Publication Data**

Clayton, John Jacob.

Radiance : ten stories / John J. Clayton.

p.    cm.

ISBN 0-8142-0779-0 (cl : alk. paper). —

ISBN 0-8142-0780-4 (alk. paper)

1. Jews—United States—Social life and customs—Fiction.

2. Jewish families—United States—Fiction.    I. Title.

PS3553.L388R33    1988

813'.54—dc21    97-46015

CIP


Text and jacket design by Paula Newcomb.


Typeset in Minion by Wilsted & Taylor Publishing Services.


Printed by Braun-Brumfield, Inc.


The paper used in this publication meets
the minimum requirements of the American
National Standard for Information Sciences—
Permanence of Paper for Printed Library Materials.

ANSI Z39.48-1992.


9 8 7 6 5 4 3 2

# Acknowledgments

Stories in this collection originally appeared in the following journals:

*Agni:* "History Lessons," "The Man Who Could See Radiance"
*Fiction:* "Talking to Charlie," "Old Friends" (under the title "Secret Lives")
*Georgia Review:* "Open-Heart Surgery"
*The Journal:* "Glory"
*Tri-Quarterly:* "Time Exposure"
*Virginia Quarterly Review:* "Dance to the Old Words"

"Talking to Charlie" was also reprinted in *O. Henry Prize Stories,* 1995

*for Sharon, for Aaron, for Sasha,*
*for Josh, for Laura, for Jed, for Lucie*

# Contents

## Talking to Charlie

*It* begins as the old story, I've told so many stories of divorce and pain: Six months back, David Kahn read by accident the wrong letter, and it was as if he'd already known, as if he finally had to open the door to the closet where the monster squatted. His wife in love with somebody, somebody brilliant, supervisor of her cases as a therapist. This guy also happened to be David's tennis partner. And in a rage, as if surprised, as if betrayed, as if such a thing had never entered his mind, he packed up, moved to a motel, drank—and fell apart.

The usual divorce story, dismal, of pain and humiliation, his family broken, ahh, you could write it yourself. Then David takes a leave from his high-powered job—selling mainframes and networks for corporations—drops everything, to live the winter like a monk at his cottage in Truro, on Cape Cod.

Why is he leaving? Revulsion, he'd tell you, for the whole megillah. Secretly, he's in panic for his life. And maybe, too, he knows, could even tell you, he's leaving out of spite; he's punishing Sarah. All these years, he's been a Good Provider. While she became the intellectual, the Ph.D. psychologist, he provided. Let somebody else do the providing.

But there's more to it. There's this. He isn't willing to be bullied anymore by the vague dream of making it, sick of working so hard—working not just to succeed but to make himself worthy in his own eyes, or really in his dead father's eyes—ghost father from childhood. What he really wants, David, is just to clear the books, to live an honorable life.

In my story he stops drinking, gets into shape. In Truro, early spring, he plants a garden: It makes him happy, on knees in old jeans, to break up the cold, sandy soil with garden fork, mix in bags of peat moss, topsoil, manure. Occupational therapy.

Big chest, heavy shoulders—funny to think of a guy like him on his knees with a young plant between his fingers, planting, then patting down the soil. A big man, David played high school football, went to Deerfield Academy for a thirteenth year on a football scholarship. Though it was track he was really good at— always a man who lugged weights: the hammer throw, the shot put, the discus. A lot of guys still take him for an athlete with his big frame and heavy neck. But since the time in the hospital for his back, he feels like a sand castle against an incoming tide, the way his chest has started to slip and sink. Bags under his eyes, and the skin between eyelids and eyebrows beginning to go limp; hair graying and the gray strands lightening, growing light as smoke, angel hair—silly when it isn't combed into place.

The gardening calms him, the beach runs clean out his head. He doesn't think so much about Sarah and Nick. Gulls and terns and the spastic little sandpipers rise up as he lumbers their way. He watches for seaweed hiding glass or shells that could cut his feet. But soon his mind falls away, the watching happens without him. A dream is how it feels. And now he begins to get peculiar intimations, as he's chopping onions, say, that everything has happened beyond his willing. Intimations that these past months of pain, the dream-maker, dream-writer, knew all along where David was going.

Climbing to the top of the dunes, he can see more than a mile of beach. Cracking explosions of surf—small charges going off together all along the beach—and then the hiss of water rushing to the high-tide line.

It scares him a little, becoming aware of this . . . presence, this dreamer of David's own life. His scriptwriter. Night of a full moon, and David wonders whose hands he's in. If, just maybe, the hands might be tender, holding him, not dangling him like a puppet but holding, and he could relax and let the guy take over.

The point is, David says to himself, that if there's a script beyond my making, he, the scriptwriter, has never *not* been in charge. It was illusion that I, David Kahn, was accomplishing anything with my struggling. I enacted, I never acted. My whole life, the dream provided a script. That's it exactly, he thinks, as he hunts driftwood for his evening fire.

And so, walking the dunes, David becomes aware of this presence he's joined to as if there were an invisible filament carrying messages between them. He talks to the presence. It's a little like the times he used to talk to God. His mother would take him to the synagogue after his father left for work Saturday morning, and he'd get sleepy and ride the waves of the old men's chantings. He didn't mind staying. But when she recited the Kaddish for her mother and father, she made him leave. Why? Was it superstition that she herself would die if he were there when she remembered a parent? Or did she not want him to see her weep? When he came back, he found her eyes red. Was she crying for her parents—or for her failure of a life? And he, unable to change her life or be her life, he stood in the marble lobby talking to God.

Now he talks to nobody, to the sky. He ought to be talking to Charlie, negotiating with Charlie Bausch, his immediate boss and his mentor at Data Management, to go back to work. Sooner or later, he'll need the money. And he'll need the work.

I tell about David, this man struggling then letting go of the need to struggle. He's ruined his days and nights trying to be worthy. Now he knows, it's this trying that is the problem, his belief in his sickness that is his sickness, the belief that his life is in his hands. And feeling now that his tense hands on the wheel give only an illusion of control—like "driving" a roller-coaster car—ahh, he lets go.

And now, magically, the story wants to move toward restoration: his family restored to him. I can feel that kind of story humming in his head. I can sense it in my own prose, sense my tenderness for David. Peaceful, he'll return to Boston, win back his wife—as if he's getting into shape for *her*—and enter a new life.

I don't trust this story.

He imagines himself at peace, imagines himself *into* peace. I write wanting—who wouldn't?—that peace for myself. The story is my own prayer to let go. To put myself in God's hands. I've never been able to let go, to quiet myself. Peace? You wish, buddy. You wish. Still, the story is true; I've felt the way David feels; there are times you float above the issues that have been clinging to you like a thick web; you know, deeply, that you've spun the web yourself, and it's not even real, it's a hologram, you can step through it and away anytime you feel like it. You needed the web. For what?—for something. I remember I sat once with a friend and felt touched by the sunlight, greenly iridescent through the plants at the window, and I didn't have to do a thing, nothing, just *be*. But a feeling like that, it comes, it goes, it's not final—New Life—God knows.

So David *wishes* it were his new life. I've wished it for him. In a sense, I'm the dreamer he's thinking about. And I'm imagining a dreamer dreaming *me*. I understand why they're so seductive,

David's imaginings: they let me see the scripts of the culture as God. No need then for a ride into the dark.

But I have to take courage and ride whatever words I can find down into the dark at the bottom of the dark. I take to my heart the old myth, everybody's old thumping heart-hunger turned myth, that there be a quest. Saying that, I see myself with a paper sword on a horse made out of words. I must want to mock this quest, its pretentiousness. But that mockery is like the dog at the mouth of darkness. One more thing to get past.

Riding down into the dark, not up toward the light. But believing in the light, that the light is there, crusted over, a pulsing jewel down at the bottom of the dark, hidden to keep the searcher safe—its danger is its core; it's nothing if not dangerous; hidden also to keep the jewel itself safe, keep it from being ruined by the wrong finder.

I'm talking about the wrong finder within my own ruined self, the fat one, the exploiter, willing to turn anything into grub. The point of the hardship in the quest is to force the self to burn in a refiner's fire, so that the soul that finds the pulsing jewel is worthy of receiving it, will make good use of it. As I pray I may be, pray I will make.

And so I find my story changing. I'm telling you not about David's falling away of self but of his longing to *believe* that he can disentangle himself from himself by himself, can ride the tails of some holy Presence. How can he, any more than I can? But the quiet is something good. He stands, thick-bodied ex-jock, winded from his morning run, at the highest point of the dunes in Truro, looking like a god over the world south toward Wellfleet, the world north toward Provincetown, beach and ocean spread out eighty feet below him, and he doesn't need to make a single business call or smile a single business smile.

And the feeling he had just a few weeks before—that his

whole life was over, this fabrication of marriage and family fallen like a house of cards, that it would be a relief to jerk the wheel of his BMW just slightly, ah, just the least bit—why, that feeling seems now as if it belonged to somebody else. He, David, is the actor who played that role, suffered through those pages in the script, and now he's inside his own skin, open to the next scene that's handed him before the shooting.

Last night I dreamed I was at an A.A. meeting—it was called that in the dream, but the room was filled with the wrecked, with hopeless alcoholics, not recovering alcoholics, and I, though not in my awake life a drinker, was on my knees in prayer, saying, "I can't do it alone, I'm in Your hands." And that's it: different as I am from David, I long the same longing, to reshape my clay. But I can't do it alone, David can't do it alone.

Not completely alone, David goes to the next town, to Wellfleet, for dinner, sits at a bar drinking seltzer and watching the Celtics. He talks trades, injuries, coaching with some of the regulars. But that's not people you work with or live with. If I'm going to imagine him into peace, and so imagine my own peace, it will have to come because he works or lives or prays peacefully with other people. Then who? Maybe a woman he meets?—but no—he did that when he was first separated.

He remembers the turmoil after he found out about Sarah, the nights of no sleep in the expensive motel, the drinking, the wreck he needed to become in order to dramatize and therefore feel some control over the pain. And then that terrible night in New York when he went to bed with a lovely woman, too young for him, thirty years old, a lawyer, thinking he was fooling them all, the gods of middle age, making a sneaky end run into a second youth without mortgage or two A.M. squabbles or back problems. Wild man again. Carol could save him. They made the bed rock.

But then he was awake and it was three-thirty in the morning in an unfamiliar New York apartment, and he was sick as hell, head thumping, mouth dry, not saved, a scared sick man of forty-five is what he was, in a strange bed, a stranger's bed. Tiptoeing into this stranger's kitchen, he drank orange juice out of a foreign glass at three in the morning.

So suppose it's a man at the bar he meets, big guy with red hair who asks him to help him out a couple of weeks, help him build an addition, kind of work David did summers when he was at college, and David, who'd earned a hundred thousand, hundred and twenty thousand a year plus stock options selling computer systems, likes the idea of working with his hands again, framing a building, putting in windows.

So he puts off talking to Charlie, Charlie Bausch, his boss. He works with this refugee from the sixties, thick red hair halfway down to his shoulders. Terry has a master's from Michigan in archeology but makes his living now as a carpenter.

The next week, he works with Terry on an addition that has to be finished this spring. By Thursday, they have it framed and sheathed. End of each day, he comes home aching, ragged, old jeans and work shirt musky with sweat, dusty with sawdust. Rock and roll in his head from the tinny radio that's always blasting under the whine of the circular saw. Maybe he'll live this way. He's surprised how much he cares to do a good job; surprised how much he remembers. He isn't surprised that Terry can keep working full-steam a lot longer than he can.

But sometimes, hefting two-by-fours, measuring and cutting, hammering, sweating, he realizes his body has taken over, he's home free, humming along on cruise control, something like that. This has nothing to do with *listening*. It's this presence, expressing itself through his hands, his shoulders. He's riding the waves. Secretly, he thinks that working with two-by-fours will help him find the jewel hidden in the dirt. For years he's been a *luftsmensch*, a man living in the air, living by phone and by phoniness, making money—just numbers—nothing you can touch.

So now, as he measures and planes, he is enacting a metaphor, a ritual, making a new David, till he imagines himself changed by the ritual he's hammered out. But David is still David, nothing to be done. He's a rough, kindhearted, lonely man, tired of pretending that he likes lugging two-by-fours all day. And he knows that if he came out here to live, he'd turn Terry's catch-as-catch-can operation into a serious construction business, he'd wind up selling houses instead of computers. Why bother? Still, the work has been good for him.

One night David looks into the mirror and sees less flab around his face, his body firm, old jock returning to jockdom. The sadness is still there in the bags under his eyes, sadness that he's lived the wrong life—his whole life he's worked like a horse to feel like a human being. But the peculiar understanding has calmed him—or the calming *is* the understanding: that not only does he live his life—he's been lived by it.

With this understanding, he returns to Boston quieted. No more boozing, no more catting around to show he still has the stuff. And with this quiet his new life begins.

Only begins: he has to find the way to the dark at the bottom of the dark, where long ago he buried someone with his true face, shining. Once in a while he has a glimpse of the face he buried long ago, as I have of my own self at the bottom of myself. Maybe it's easier for David, for he has less to lose. That's the point of being stripped naked, like Lear on the heath. Maybe I envy him.

If I knew how to imagine David going on from there, finding the jewel, changing in the soul, maybe I'd know how to make my own peace. But back in Brookline, in the apartment he finds not a mile from the old house, he feels less peaceful and more alone. The lovely quiet of the dunes, the sense that he was held in the hand of that benign Presence—it's hard to get it back. There's no ocean to sing to him, and sometimes he wonders, was it just a trick of consciousness, his imaginings of a presence supporting him, being spoken by his life?

He thinks about work, about talking to Charlie. Sitting at a deli on Beacon Street and poking through the want ads in the *Globe,* he finds the good jobs not all that different from his work at Data Management. Why lose what he's built? Why lose colleagues he cares about? He's watched their kids grow up.

I'm listening on headphones to the music of Thomas Tallis, mid-sixteenth-century English composer, choral music of peace and harmony, written at a time of chaos, struggle, murder, torture, poverty, and oppression. Well, what time hasn't been like that? Tallis was composing within a tradition, even while he was changing it. And underpinning the tradition was a separate world, a world of the spirit, on which he could stand while the world around him was full of murder. Where can David stand?

There are times he stands on a street corner on his way to pick up Beth at school and watches a couple of MTA cars glide by down Beacon, and suddenly he feels a hollow rush in his belly, as if he were riding a roller coaster. And he realizes there's a piece of himself standing high up above Beacon Street, looking down from a high haven.

Every other weekend, he sees Beth and Noah from Friday afternoon until Monday night. Sarah, who has a full caseload and then works at the Boston Institute for Psychotherapy some evenings, is grateful for the help. When he doesn't have them on the weekend, they're with him two nights midweek. When the kids complain about all the changing, they begin to spend alternate weeks—one week with Sarah, one with David.

Now, half the time a single parent, responsible for a ten-year-old boy, a four-year-old girl, he's got to think about making dinner for them every night, think about whether they have clean clothes for the morning. He's got to have their friends over and drive them home. Now he sees what it is to be a father.

Slow, patient, a yoga of steadiness and devotion. This is a story I trust and understand. A person changes by doing the laundry on a daily basis, by picking up the kids at school and taking them to gymnastics. This is the work. No mysteries.

But David resists this story. His new life feels full of mysteries. Something's happening I don't understand, a trick of consciousness, maybe, but it lets him float above his pain. I've always thought that the dark body, of which the person you look at in the mirror is merely an emanation, had to be restored in battle. You have to wrestle for the prize. Deny and deny until you can't deny and your face is rubbed bloody into the dirt; then raw, burnished, it shines with darkness. But as he gets used to being back, and being with the kids, David doesn't do battle: doesn't go back to work or into therapy. He hangs out; he wanders. He finds himself in a city with . . . reduced gravity. He doesn't need, the way he used to, to be weighed down, doesn't need his pain. He thinks, *It's still there, the pain. Just not so much* mine.

He takes long walks through Boston, feeling the strangeness of not working. And the part of him that's free of gravity and in touch with something beyond himself, that part begins to occupy his shoes. At this rate, he says, I'll never wear my shoes out. Someone leads, he follows, perfect dancer.

Sitting over a cup of decaf listening to Miles Davis after the kids are asleep, he gets a sudden urge to call Sarah. He doesn't call—afraid she'll take it wrong, as a sign of his longing. And he's doing all right. That same night, *she* calls, needing to talk. Can we meet? Sure, he says, I'd like that.

Is she, he wonders, going to insist on couples' therapy? Sarah is one tough insister. Well, he's not eager, but willing. He makes a mental note not to make fun of therapy, therapists, psychology in general. He and Sarah will have to be especially careful of one another's bruised places. David goes to a barber, he buys a new suit, dove gray; he's like a bridegroom getting ready for a wedding. Looking into the mirror, if he doesn't peer too closely, he likes what he sees—a ruddy, strong man in his prime. A little beefy, okay—and crude for a woman like Sarah; still, women go for him. And okay—there are the wounds: terrible, humiliating nights like the night in Bermuda when (they were making love) looking into her eyes, he saw she wasn't at home. Not even a message machine on. He ended that night alone, talking to himself in an outdoor hot tub. Marriage! The wounds and, worse, the bruises. Why else is it that before marriage and kids, we can meet each other and dance together with words, everything is tender music; then we marry and can't even buy a ticket to the dance hall?

But driving Sarah to a really good little French restaurant they both used to like, slipping the little BMW between lanes like a great jockey maneuvering a thoroughbred, he feels optimistic. He tells her how nice the garden in Truro is turning out, and she asks about those lovely words: *hollyhocks, columbine, delphinium.*

In a dark corner of the restaurant, he sits across the table with its checkered tablecloth and sips wine and leans his chin on his hands and his elbows on the table and grins like a fool at Sarah, listening to her story about Noah at gymnastics. This woman, he says to himself, so beautiful to me even now, Jewish Indian with her olive complexion and prominent nose, the heavy, lovely breasts I see with my hands' eye, and black hair curly and turbulent no matter what she does to tame it.

He sees her face now and it becomes her face at the instant after she'd given birth to Beth, and her hair, oh, was stringy, her skin bloated and her eyes giddy with joy. He'd been crying, too, crying for the newborn they'd lost two years before, crying with relief that this time it would be okay, the birth okay, Beth was going to live.

"You're looking good," he says. "Been working out, I bet."

"Not much. You look really good, yourself."

This woman, he says to himself, she's still my life. His eyes mist, he blows his nose in his table napkin, then remembers how she hates to see him do that. He laughs to make it a gag.

"So," he says after they order, "you called the meeting. You need a new computer or what? Kidding, kidding—hey, tell me, how are we doing with the kids? Pretty good, I think."

"Really, really good," she said. "It's some change. God. You remember, Davie—I'm not saying this to start anything, but—when you were home you were never home."

"I know, I know," he says.

"You were always somewhere else, always at the office, on the phone all weekend."

"You're right, you're absolutely right."

"Really, I'm happy about it—especially for Noah. He's been needing a father bad."

"I don't think I ever realized, so help me God. The kids, they've been a lot to me these past months." Been *everything*, he would have said, been my script—but he wants to come on like a man of strength, a grown-up.

"Well, it's wonderful, Davie."

"See? I can learn, Sarah. I guess I'm never going to talk about French feminist psychoanalysts, but I can learn about being a father. Maybe a husband."

She sips her wine, he's afraid to put his hand on hers. "So what do you think?" he whispers.

It takes her time to catch up to him. Then she's there, and she drops her eyes. "Oh. David, I'm a fool," she says.

"No, no—"

"Listen, you don't understand," she says. "I'm really sorry. I mean, that's not why I wanted us to talk."

"Okay. Okay. That's okay." He holds up his hands, palms out in surrender.

"No—I'm sorry. I wanted you to know—I wanted to say it face-to-face—I might get married again," she says. "I'm probably getting married, Davie. Married to Nick. So . . . we need to begin proceedings, you and me."

There's a hollow rush in his belly, and he breathes in a deep breath, and his eyes lift involuntarily into the ceiling. Only he can't lift up into a safe haven above himself, looking down on the poor sufferer. He *is* the sufferer. He's falling through a hole.

"Sure," he says. "My lawyer and your lawyer. We'll get a letter of agreement ready." Falling through a hole—or it's like his real life is a train leaving the station without him. He smiles his salesman smile and wants to drink his wine but he's afraid the glass will be shaky in his hand. At the same time, another piece of him is thinking shrewdly that if she needs an agreement so quickly, then okay, good, he'll come out of this with more than his shirt. Is she afraid, he wonders, that too long a delay and Nick might back off? Could Nick do a thing like that, the prick? He finds himself feeling protective, like a father worrying that his daughter might get hurt by a suitor. It must be a cover-up feeling, he thinks. He must be full of rage. Down and down and down he looks for it, for the rage, but all he feels is protective and full of grief and afraid she'll see. He says, "Don't worry, Sarah. I'll get my guy on it right away."

The only way he can keep from drinking now is to work out hard. He does Nautilus, takes a daily swim. The worse he feels, the more he needs the discipline. His life has imploded into a core of pain. There's nothing in him to resist gravity, to lift himself up above himself. He dances to no strange tune. His *story* collapses, and with it the David who wasn't burdened by his life, the David who enacted a dream, a script he'd been handed. It's no script. All morning he sits, like stone, like one of those meteorites in the planetarium—hot rock melted into dense, cold stone, pure weight—sits over coffee and fingers his lower lip and looks up his stocks in the *Globe*.

    This isn't what he had in mind. It's the wrong story. He's supposed to have suffered and become a changed soul with a new life. *This* grief seems a waste. There are ways to use grief, taught for thousands of years, but none of them David knows. Alone, the soul, awash in grief until half-drowned, grasps any rock it already knows. Change it wants, though still—still to be somehow familiar to itself. Maybe what is being asked instead is that the soul let go, that it become a sea creature; and it would rather die than grow gills or turn dolphin, so strange! Instead, it will pretend to change, like Proteus, the Old Man of the Sea. Wrestle with him, Menelaus was told; don't let him go no matter how he seems to change form. David, not knowing how to wrestle, sits and fingers his lower lip.

Mired in pain, maybe it's a good thing he has to begin thinking of money. He's just another guy in Massachusetts out of work. He's got money put away for the kids' education, money in an annuity, but he's been cashing in CDs and treasury notes, and it doesn't feel so romantic, so life-renewing, as it did at the beach. He can't keep stringing Data Management along, they won't hold his position open forever. Finally, he has to go back to D.M. and talk to Charlie Bausch. Driving out to 128, just as if this were a year ago and nothing had gone down, he finds himself lifting out of himself, high up above the BMW, above Route 9, and he looks down on a guy who couldn't make a new life or fix up the old one, a guy who was broken the way everybody gets broken.

Everybody, everybody, it's like being popped onto the board of a pinball machine and—whew!—missing the holes, one, two, three. You don't die in somebody's war or gas chamber, you don't get cancer or AIDS, your kids don't Godforbid get childhood leukemia, you don't wind up in a dead-end job and some roach-infested apartment in Chelsea, but the board is slanted, and sooner or later—wait—there'll be a hole for you.

D.M. feels strange to him, maybe most strange because nobody seems to notice anything unusual about his being back. He waves at Ed McKitterick, at Ginny Shepherd with the lovely doe eyes—all these years he's wanted just to touch her face and to bless her or be blessed. He keeps walking, successful-salesman grin stuck on his face.

Sales works out of an open-plan office, half a football field of space, columns at regular intervals but cubicles every which way, a maze of cubicles. As he threads his usual path, he hears a guffaw. Stephen Anapulsky bursts out of his cubicle laughing, Sid Langdorf out of *his*—

"That clown, he turned the messages on my screen upside down, the clown!"

His office is still untouched, the drawers still stuffed with his papers, with old snapshots of the kids. He writes a note to the custodian: PLEASE CLEAN UP. THANKS! And he heads for his meeting with Charlie Bausch.

Too heavy still, though he's lost maybe thirty pounds, Charlie carries his weight like a tired old sailor lugging a duffle. He limps a little, but David's always thought of it as a royal swagger. As if there's something dignified the way Charlie Bausch hefts the extra weight and the tired bones.

They've never really become friends, but for fifteen years now, Charlie Bausch has been his mentor in the company. *I made some success, where did I take it but to Charlie?* Old salesman himself, Charlie taught him shrewdness, and often, middle of a sales presentation, David finds Charlie inhabiting his body, finds himself mellowing down, slowing his gestures, slowing his voice like a record going from 45 rpm to 33, down to Charlie's courteous gravel tones. I think what he does is he gets clients into a kind of hypnotic trance, a place where they feel so comfortable that they're open to persuasion.

Especially since Charlie's heart attack a few years ago, David has found his own heart open to him. The guy can get a little boring, but boring isn't so bad. If Charlie can't stop talking about the international bond market or about his granddaughter in Phoenix, what the hell.

He looks puffy and dark under the eyes, Charlie.

They talk, as they have a couple of times over the phone, about the sales that David left unfinished. "You know about

Polaroid coming through," Charlie says. "That commission is yours, you know." Then Charlie tilts way back in his chair, feet go up, pencil between his two forefingers like a bridge over a precipice—a posture that means, *I'm gonna philosophize, Dave;* that really means, *I'm gonna sell you something.*

"Dave," he says, "I can understand a guy going through confused times, he goes off and puts himself together. I respect that. A retreat's a great thing. The Catholics are no dopes, they've been successful a long time with this retreat business."

"You've been very kind to me, Charlie."

"Kind? I've been grooming you. You know that. I don't want to see you lose it all. Forget the Catholics. Think of it this way," Charlie says, his voice slowing down and, like the voice on a tape recorder played half-speed, dropping into a lower register. "You got knocked around the first half, so you rested in the locker room. Now you suit up. . . . You used to play fullback, am I right?—you get back on the field and you play to win."

"But suppose," David says, falling into the slow melancholy of Charlie Bausch's talk, "suppose you don't care about the game, suppose it's the wrong game?"

"Dave, listen, listen, Dave: It's the only game in town."

David considers this. He wishes he could ask Charlie why it was a game worth playing, but Charlie doesn't have answers like that. Besides, David knows it's a ritual, this talk. There's really no need to convince him of anything, he walked in here convinced that he has no other option. Just walking in, no matter how kind Charlie is, has got to feel like a defeat.

"The way I see it," Charlie says in a kind of singsong, "everything got sour for you when Sarah kicked you out. Your work, whatever. Are you kidding me? If you really hated your work, you couldn't do the job you do. Am I right? Tell me, 'You're right, Charlie.' "

"You *are* right, Charlie. I'm a salesman."

"I know I'm right. How many times'd you win the special

parking place, Salesman of the Month? For christsakes, you practically owned the slot. You're a better salesman than I ever was."

"That's bullshit."

"But you're forty-five years old, maybe it's time to get you out
of the trenches. Like me. Okay, here's my offer. Regional Sales
Manager is opening up. You want it?"

David looks into Charlie's tired eyes and solemnly nods.

"Surprised you, huh? See, the only way I could sell your goddamn desertion to the big guys, I said, 'Kahn is sniffing out a
management position.' They came through. We'll talk details
another time," Charlie says, voice lifting. "Let's you and me go get
some dessert to celebrate. To hell with the cholesterol."

David drives Beth and Noah down to Truro. They're lucky: it's a
sunny Friday afternoon and promises to be sunny all weekend.
Late June. Cape light. A few of the tulips are still blooming, waving in the wind, making the old house look as if somebody lives
there, it's not a summer rental. A pioneer columbine is flowering, and the bleeding heart is fuller than it has a right to be this
first year. Look, look. To humor his dad, Noah looks—and sighs
ironically at the way his dad always makes him look at growing
things. He's developed a half-scowl David feels partly responsible
for, as much a defense as the squint of eyes against the sun. But his
eyes—dark brown, deep—are still exposed, tender. It's why he
needs the scowl. Beth sniffs a tulip and comes away disappointed.
But she spots a toad and, exploding in one of her thick, hoarse
laughs, she makes a grab. It's a wonder to David, the delicacy of
her skin, so fine you can see the vein, blue, of her forehead, and
then her heft and this laugh of hers.

They carry in suitcases and groceries, soon they're hiking the
sand trail over the dunes to the beach. Noah adores David's cellular phone. "Can we take it along? Will it work from the beach?"

"Can I call Mommy and she can listen to the ocean?" Beth
wants to know.

"We'll try." David hooks it on the belt of his jeans.

At ten, Noah isn't too old to be excited about his dad's new job. He asks, "Will you be on the road a lot?"

"Less than I used to. The money's less, too. . . . Beth?—Careful of the prickers on the bushes, Beth."

"How come?" Noah asks. "You'll be top guy."

"But I'm not out there as much doing the selling and pulling down the big commissions. You know what commissions are?"

Noah nods. Beth says, "What are commissions?" But before he has to answer, she sees a rabbit and runs after it, yelling, "Bunny, bunny, bunny!"

"Still, it'll be better, Noah. There's stock options. And I'll have more time with you and Beth."

"No-eee, No-eee!" Beth calls, her name for her brother since she could speak at all. "Find me, No-eee."

"Regional Manager! *Yes!*" Noah says, doing a victory dance for his father.

"I'll tell you the God's honest truth," his father says. "I wouldn't be disappointed if you did something else entirely."

"Like what?"

"Like . . . anything. What can you imagine yourself doing?"

Noah, not wanting to think, runs off through the scrub oak and squat pine of the outer Cape. He pretends to search for Beth.

When David gets to the top of a high dune, he finds a strong offshore wind that drives through his zipper and down his neck. He can lean into the wind; it holds him up. And he closes his eyes and imagines he's hang gliding, all two hundred pounds of him floating on this wind. He hears Beth's singsong and Noah's shout.

And his elbow bumps the cellular phone, so he imagines it's ringing, because how else *can* he get in touch these days? The presence he'd listened to, it hasn't been present, maybe he's been too busy, moving into his new office, making calls, making meetings, making a living if not exactly a life. So it makes crazy sense

to him that if he wants to get in touch again, it should be with
this phone.

When it rings, wherever he is, it connects him to his ordinary
world, there's no getting away from it anywhere anymore. So he
imagines a different ring—oh, it's like little bells—and looking
around to make sure the kids aren't in sight, he takes the phone
off his belt and says, "David Kahn here." But there's no voice from
some other end. "I know," he whispers over the rush of wind,
"that even when I hear nothing, I'm saying what you're telling me
and doing what you'd have me do. Isn't that right?"

"What, Daddy?" Beth's there; she holds onto his leg, this
small chunk of wild-haired girl, attaching him solidly to the
dune.

"I'm just pretend-talking. . . . Hello, hello," he says into the
phone. "You want to talk to Bev? *Bev*—I don't know anyone by
that name. Sorry."

"*Beth*, it's for *me*, I'm Beth."

"Oh, it's *Beth* you want. Well, here."

"Hello," Beth says, taking the phone. "Well, I'd love to come
to your party. . . . All right. . . . They want to talk to you."

David takes the phone. "Oh, I see. Well, we will," he says to
the phone. And to Beth he says, "Dance. They said we have to
dance." Still holding the phone, David dances his daughter at the
top of the dune, round and round, oom-pah-pah, as if he's got no
choice; and in the middle of the dance he feels it coming back, the
connection, the presence, as if he's a fish at the end of an invisible
line, and he's so into his dance he doesn't know Noah's there till
the kid says, "Who're you talking to, Dad? You talking to Mom?"

"No," David says, phone to his ear, "I'm talking to Charlie.
Just talking to Charlie."

Because it's the same, he thinks, as long as you do the dance.
David dances, and me, I watch him do his dance, while I do my
own, hoping that I can hear the music, and that, at least for a
while, David's dance can take me home.

# *History Lessons*

*eter* at my side, I walk up Columbus Avenue, where I walked as a child—only then, what was it but a grubby street of bars and walk-ups with black iron fire escapes over their facades, deli on one side (smell of brine of the pickle barrel) and, across the street, huge seedy residential hotel everyone knew was seeded with whores and dope fiends. Close my eyes, I can see Columbus the old way, bleak but exciting, two-way traffic those days, my father holding my arm to steer me past the drunks. I remember a man flung out horizontal from a saloon. He flew slow-motion high through the air like some anti-Superman and ended in the gutter, blood turning his face into a mask, as if all the skin were stripped away. I even remember his giant nose—well, I'd seen him before, poor bastard, the nose swollen, deeply pocked, and my mother, I remember I was walking with my mother, she nudged but didn't point and whispered, "You see? That's *syphilis*. You wouldn't understand. Godforbid *you* should end like that."

I don't tell any of this to Peter, my seventeen year old. Both of

us in casual slacks and good sweaters, an adult victory—he's usually in torn jeans and rock-band tee shirts. As far as his mother
knows, we're in New York to look at colleges—and we have been
to Columbia, my alma mater. But in fact, I'm walking down this
new Columbus with him because he asked to see where I grew up.
I tell him that these stores and restaurants are all new, but I don't
tell him how *much* the street has changed. How dark it was. How
dirty and exciting. I don't tell him of the Irish kids who beat up
the Jewish kids from the big apartment buildings. I walked wary.

He's wearing a book bag on his back; he's holding a micro
tape recorder in his hand, his stepfather's. Making it an *interview*
lets it be comfortable for him; he knows I don't talk about my
childhood. But as a project in family history for his high school
history class it's okay, he's not just asking intimate questions.
He's heard "everything," he says, about his mother's childhood
in Colorado, about his grandparents—his mother's parents—
and about *their* parents, a merchant family in Sweden. "Now it's
your turn," he kidded me on the phone. "You know, Dad—I
don't know a whole lot about you."

I laugh on cue. I've heard his mother's stories about family
skiing adventures in Colorado. I don't have such stories.

Columbus, I tell him, it's the street I knew, a street strange to
me. "The old neighborhood's gone—and just as well, Peter. But I
still know New York. You stick with me, we're going to cook this
town up for dinner. You're with a native." I don't tell him how the
glory dreams brewed in my childhood Manhattan are gone too,
along with the brewers who stirred those dreams. I don't tell him
I'm a native who never comes back; if I have a business meeting in
the city, I'm in and out the same day. I don't talk family; I give him
a history lesson:

*"A hundred years ago, this was way out of town,"* I say into his
tape recorder. I can feel myself making grand myth out of history.
*"Sheep grazed in Central Park. Then they built the Dakota and a
couple of other big apartment buildings on Central Park West and*

*Broadway. Then rows of brownstones for the people in the offices. Later, Columbus went downhill. When I was a kid, it was a peculiar kind of slum, because the stores still catered to the fancy apartment houses. Mostly Jews. Walk-ups housed the Irish and Greek and Italians; later, Puerto Ricans. Then, 'urban renewal'—a phony name to cover up what they were doing—getting rid of the Hispanics by getting rid of their homes. When I grew up, it started to get chic, Peter. It's gentrified now,"* I tell him. *"Ethnic restaurants, fashions. The gentry. Same beer's expensive now. There's history: price of a beer went up."*

He laughs. "Dad, I don't call Columbus exactly fancy. I mean *look*."

I look. Sure. Street torn up, stores out of business, same black fire escapes with dead plants, filthy windows, shabby walk-up rooms behind. Still, there's a Laura Ashley on Seventy-ninth, there's a twenty-story apartment building.

I thumb at the ponderous brownstone original building of the American Museum of Natural History. Peter's got his eyes open. Seeing through his eyes or what I imagine to be his eyes, I try to dream a kind of city radiance into being.

Not glory—it's something else I hunger for now. Imagine you're walking along Columbus thinking, say, of buying apples at a corner fruit stand and a woman walks by holding spring flowers (although it's fall, a clean bright day) and takes you with her by the heart so that you follow her with your eyes, forgetting to be embarrassed in front of your grown son. And you're nudged awake, especially because you imagine *he's* nudged awake, and now the street begins to resonate in you, bus groans and stench and a little boy yelling, "Hey, Mommy, Mommy, wait!" while Mommy, fed up with his dawdling, hurries on ahead. You hear the thump of hip-hop, full bass beating out of the open window of a car; the throbbing cry of an ambulance. Somebody should make music of it, like the Elizabethan songs based on street cries of London.

Of course, that music isn't radiance, I don't mean that—but as the city becomes real and suddenly you forget all about your apple, that's the way radiance dissolves desire, when, for a moment, wings brush your face, when for a moment you recognize that the ginkgo tree bends just that way, no other, that even a dog on a leash walks in inward pulse of Being; that everything, even that woman talking so intently to herself, is charged with the life of its own making, life beyond your making and using.

It's that sense of being inside Being that Peter lends me as we walk. I feel a flowering of my spirit usually inaccessible to me— now it's gone again, because there's so much I'm not saying to him it crams up inside, gridlock, not all that hard to say, but no need to dump it on him. How sorry I am we don't see each other much. At the Stage Deli I'd asked, "How's Emma? You still close friends?" "Emma?" he laughed. "Dad! She's out in California. I haven't seen Emma in over a year." So I'm afraid to ask questions I should know the answers to. I moved away. We live in different cities and what the hell, I know, weekends a teenager needs his friends, but how sorry I am. So I bore him with questions not my real concern—whether or not to apply to Cornell, is he getting behind in his AP class in calculus? He rolls his eyes, good-humoredly enough. "Dad, come on—will you please get off my back?"

I hold up my palms in surrender, I smile but feel I've failed us again. I don't say how much I love it that the idea for this trip came from him. I was the one who called up and said, "What about a weekend in New York, Peter? We can do a Broadway show?" But he was the one said, "Sure. Great. But, Dad, what I really want to do, Dad—I want to see the places you grew up."

It's late; we spent too long at the Stage Delicatessen over pastrami and pickles, then walking past Lincoln Center and up Columbus; so before we get to my old street I veer off at Eighty-first and cross Central Park, past my playground surrounded by black iron bars,

past the runners, bikers, roller bladers—Central Park parade.
Past the pond, little castle I laid siege to; past Cleopatra's Needle
to the Met. After school, those days my mother stayed in her
room, cursing, in Yiddish, Hitler or her life, when the apartment
felt as if all the air had been sucked out, here is where I came to
breathe—even as a nine year old. A city kid who'd never seen a
harvest; still, I felt at home when I climbed the grand stairs to the
sunlight of Breughel's *Harvesters*.

Peter looks up at the great triple-vaulted ceiling as if this were
St. Peter's in Rome, grand and somehow sacred.

I cop a look at him aslant. He's bigger than me already, over
six foot, but he walks so gracefully I wonder where he got his
grace. His mother, I suppose. Same place he got his blonde good
looks. Me, I'm built like a wrestler, I move like a wrestler, my hair
thick, curly, once black.

"Wicked huge," he says, looking up, and I laugh at the language, and he knows that and grins.

"You've been here before, haven't you?"

"*I* can't remember," he says. "Not for years and years I
think"—and he smiles his extraordinary smile. Not his polite
smile or his happy smile or his ironic grin. This one's like a love-
gift, not just to me, love-gift to the world, and it dissolves the need
for questions and answers.

We climb the great staircase, but at the top there's a dead wall
that doesn't belong, cutting off the gallery where Breughel's *Harvesters* hung. We wander the labyrinth of rooms until we find it;
he likes the color, I tell him I used to lose myself inside that sunlit
field. I don't tell him why.

I try not to lecture. We look at young Rembrandt, then old
Rembrandt, and I talk changes in brush stroke to avoid talking
about the real changes—what life did to Rembrandt, what it's going to do to Peter. I don't want to come on as some middle-aged
tragedy soul, because that's not the father he needs me to be. His
stepfather, administrator in a small Vermont hospital, is a good

guy and reliable, but dreary, bland, and I figure Peter needs a more exciting model. We go from canvas to canvas in the room of Degas pastels, where I can talk upbeat about "vitality" and "experiment."

Now we wander through little rooms of late medieval paintings, and looking up I find he's gone, and I'm uneasy—we made no backup plans to meet if we got separated. He's a big kid, I'm not worried; still, unease roils in my stomach as I jog through the maze again. It's like fast-forwarding through the history of Western art the way paintings blur past. And there he is, next to El Greco's *View of Toledo,* he's looking at the picture with a girl, older than he is I think, and I see his shining—I wonder if *she* sees it, if other people *get* it, this shining he does, something he *does,* that emanates from him, for me at least, a thing of the eyes, I suppose, but it seems to be generated by the whole of him.

I keep my distance, but he spies me and waves me over.

Waves me over! Used to be, when I drove up to see him in Brattleboro, he wouldn't let me near his friends. "Dad, just pull up here. I'll walk the rest of the way. Okay?" But now—now I come up to him, and he says, "Dad, we were talking about movies. What's that early Scorsese film we saw?"

"*Mean Streets?*"

"Right. *Mean Streets,*" he says to the girl.

"Oh, I *love* that movie," she says. "Well, I love *Scorsese,*" she laughs. I feel the affectation and don't care. I'm taken with her smile. She tosses a wave of blonde hair back from her eyes. The gesture reminds me of Peter's mother when I first knew her. Blonde like Peter, girl with long legs. A pretty girl, and that she seems interested in Peter pleases me. "You go to college in New York?"

"I'm still in *high* school," she says, and her eyes half close with the tedium and embarrassment. "I'm a senior."

"You want to join us for a cappuccino?" I ask her.

"Oh I can't, I'm sorry. Maybe I'll see you. I'm meeting a friend at the restaurant. But thanks. Thank you. Really."

Peter says it was nice talking, and when we're alone he stares up at the El Greco. "God. That's some weird city," he says. "A ghost city. . . . Nice!"

"I always liked it." We walk to the restaurant. "So, you dig that girl?"

"Oh, Dad!" Not needing to understand exactly how he's making fun of me, I grin.

There's not much of a line—it's after lunchtime—we sit over cappuccino and biscuit, and I remember the bronze boys lifting arcs of water from their penises, circles on the surface of the pool expanding and conjoining. Now it's just columns and white tablecloths. "Before we go, I want you to see the American wing."

"Fine. But we want to see the house you grew up in, the school you went to. Right? There's still plenty of time, Dad."

"That makes me feel real good—that you *ask*. It does. But you know—it's nothing special, where I grew up. Nothing special at all. A third-rate apartment building on a lousy side street. I want to go back up to Columbia, really check it out, maybe you'll apply. I guess I'd be proud. And I want to take you downtown, show you the *real* New York!"

"That's okay, Dad. *Special*. I don't expect anything special. I told you—it's my history I'm after. Okay?"

There's a woman by herself a couple of tables over, my age, mid-forties, new kind of mid-forties. When I was a kid, a woman forty-five was a dreary, pudgy matron, permed hair, dead clothes. This woman pulsates shrewdness and sexual stuff. Her hair, auburn flecked with gray, is cropped pixie-style around her head. Its severity shows off her strong-boned, suntanned face. Her eyes, calm, are the eyes of a woman who knows what she wants.

"Dad, you're staring."

I guess I am. I grin and look down at my cappuccino and eat my biscuit. Odd. Usually, I don't mind if Peter sees me interested in a woman—so long his mom and I have been apart. This time I feel flustered. I keep her face lit up behind my eyes, and as I do, it changes, and now I get it, I get it and look up. "Excuse me, Peter." I stroll over. "Sylvia?"

I can see she doesn't know me. But looking into her face, I'm sure. "I'm sorry?" she says.

"Sylvia. I'm Daniel Rose. We were kids, I used to come over to your house; your father, the doctor, he played in a quartet. Thursday nights, remember?"

"Oh, Daniel—Daniel, for godsakes!" She laughs and stands, a small woman—I'd forgotten that—strong and lean, a runner, I'll bet, wearing a mauve cashmere sweater as if needing the sweater to soften her act. She squeezes both my hands in both of hers. "Oh my God."

"Your father played viola, right? When Joseph Roismann was in town, he'd come by and sit in. Out of friendship."

"That's right. And the cellist was my Uncle Leon."

"He had long hair."

"Oh! Very long, for those days."

"He was a truly terrible cellist." We laugh together. I remember Uncle Leon's hair wild over his eyes, making him feel, I think, like a passionate, serious musician. "But I loved those nights," I tell her. "I can see your father getting furious, stomping his foot to keep poor Leon in time. . . . "

Peter comes over. "Sylvia, this is my son," I say. "This is Peter, my son. Peter, I knew this woman, I knew Sylvia Gold when I was your age. It's been twenty, twenty-five years since we lost touch."

I go back to our table to get our trays and give them time to meet, and I watch her face, as I always do when I introduce Peter to someone.

We sit together. She says, "Your father and I were good good friends. *So* long ago. . . . I have a son and daughter," she says to me, "both grown up. My girl is married already."

"And your father?" I ask. "What a sweet man. What a dear man."

She nods. "Dad died three years ago. My mother's moved to Florida. And—*your* father?"

"*Many* years ago. Well. . . . You know he was much older than my mother."

"He did what he could," she says solemnly. "I mean *after-ward*." And I see out of the corner of my eye that Peter's curious. I know without seeing.

"He tried to be a good father," I say mechanically. And the snakes in my belly start their old shameful gyrations. Shame-ful—I'm ashamed to be at their mercy like this, and I try to give Sylvia a Look, but she doesn't see.

She says, "I remember like it was yesterday."

"Yes . . . yes. So—are you living in New York—all this time in New York?"

Now she gets the drift, and she changes her tune, begins to tell me about her career as a historian, about her book on nineteenth-century women's diaries and photographs. I tell her about my work healing sick companies, growing healthy ones. I tell her about Peter's history project. This lights her up; she wants to ask more.

I exchange glances with Peter, and I tell her, "We've got to go, I'm afraid. Well, you look lovely, Syl."

"Oh. I'm . . . really sorry," she says. I know what she means. I nod—it's okay, it's okay—and shake her hand and look around for the best way through the tables; we stand, and there's that girl again, the blonde girl we met upstairs, she's looking all around and Sylvia stands and waves her over.

Now we laugh, the four of us, and go through three minutes of a flustered dance. My goddaughter, Sylvia says, Alicia O'Con-nor. The daughter of my dearest friend, she says, Ruth's daughter

. . . and Peter's grinning and they shake hands, Peter and Alicia, can you imagine, how funny . . . and now the two of them go off for pastries.

"I *am* sorry," Sylvia says again. "So Peter doesn't know?"

"He knows she's dead."

"I suppose that's enough. . . . "

"I've always thought so. I suppose I intend to tell him someday. But even then—why?"

She nods and stops nodding. Now: "What are you afraid of?"

"Nothing. Nothing, really. But why? What for?"

"Of course I understand. I do understand."

I take that in. "Yes. How wonderful you were to me!"

"Not so wonderful. I felt for you. Daniel? I *felt* for you."

"You were what?—fourteen, fifteen. And we weren't even dating. It's unusual for kids to feel like that for other people."

"Oh, I don't think so. No, I don't find that to be true at all. You were a person with heart. You *were*. And now Peter, too. I'm sure of it. Don't you feel that about him?"

I feel as if I've revealed some defect in my way of seeing, in my heart now. "I'm saying it wasn't . . . *ordinary,* that's all. I want to say thank you, I've never forgotten, Sylvia. You listened, you didn't try to smooth it over. My father needed me to tell him it was all *okay.*"

"Your poor father."

"Poor everyone. Right? Poor goddamn *every*one." We sit there, mourning. Finally, I say, "And your husband—what does he do?"

"I'm no longer married. Not for many years. I'm Sylvia Gold again."

The kids come back, Peter's carrying Alicia's tray and they're talking as they come, talking rock groups and sitcoms to check out each other's taste. I tell Sylvia that I, too, have been divorced for a number of years. And right away I find myself playing with the idea of seeing Sylvia again, of starting something—as I do so often when I see an attractive woman. And I think how automatic it is for me and in this case what a joke—because even when we were young she and I never thought of ourselves that way. We talked for hours when we could get away with it, we came here to the Metropolitan, we sneaked into second acts of Broadway shows. I told her things in Village coffee shops.

She must see something in my face, I must have given myself away, because what she says now is so clearly for information, clearly so I won't make a mistake. "You'll have to come over and see me. And meet Alicia's mother. Meet *Ruth*. We *live* together, we have for five years."

"Sylvia's my co-Mom, as well as my godmother," Alicia laughs, and it's obviously a well-used line. Now, maybe embarrassed, she touches Sylvia's arm and says, "Mostly, she's my friend. She's always been."

"Well, you're lucky. I know. She was *my* friend," I say. "In a way, she still is. You still are," I say. "Funny how it is, how nearly all the cells in our bodies change every few years—not to mention marriages and careers and children—and here we are, still the same people. You're still Sylvia. Or I'm the same, I mean I see you the same. More and more this afternoon, your face; it's like a special effect in a movie, the way your face has turned into the face of the girl I knew."

"Will you stop by? There's something I'd love to show you," Sylvia says, putting her hand on mine. I understand the gesture. Now she can chance it.

"What about tomorrow? We have a show tonight."

"Please. Tomorrow. Come for brunch about eleven. Will you do that?"

I feel a little uneasy walking back across the park now that the sun has slipped behind the rooftops of the grand apartment buildings of Central Park West. Looking back we see the upper stories of the buildings along Fifth Avenue glowing. When I'm in the park, old habit—I keep my eyes open for danger. But it's still bright out, and we're not alone. Strollers. A karate class all in white. Homeless men, strollers loaded with plastic bags. Warm fall day, Peter's feeling expansive. He stops in the middle of the Great Lawn, looks around him 360, and says, "In-*cred*-ible!" And he spins as he used to when he was ten, arms spread, head back, floating, letting Manhattan issue from his fingers.

"So how did you lose touch?" he asks, returning to earth.

"With Sylvia? Oh. She went away to college when I went to Columbia. Then I went away to grad school. Then your mother and I moved away and . . . we made different lives, that's all. It happens. You'll see."

He laughs. "Dad! I wasn't criticizing you. You're so funny."

I show him the rocks I used to climb; once they seemed like a cliff, now a small granite outcropping. We leave the park and walk up Central Park West and down a side street to the small apartment building where I grew up. The same and not the same. I remember *shabby:* the street littered, the canopy torn, tile of the lobby filthy, the walls faded and soiled, the enamel-metal door of the elevator scored with curses. It's not fancy now but clean, cared for. I don't say any of this to Peter—just tell him, into the tape recorder, *"This is where we played stoop ball. And Chinese handball! A lost art."* I describe how the hollow rubber ball had to bounce. I show him the brownstones along the street, nice now, kept up; those days, before they were bought up and refurbished, walk-ups of the poor.

"So? What was it like, you and your parents?"

I shrug. I point out our windows on the facade. Our building had an elevator, but the line between us and them was too thin. I hear the words, *You see how he makes me live? You see?*

What can I do about that now?

And the poor giant roaring in pain, roaring at me out of his pain, poor father I wished dead for her, for both of us. She wanted her real life back. As if there were some Real Life, meant for her in heaven, stolen by Hitler, stolen by my father.

"So your father—" Peter prods "—your father sold dresses."

"Wholesale. He sold for a manufacturer. It was a struggle."

"And your mom? You never said."

"Mothers didn't usually *do* back then," I explain.

"I know. But wasn't she educated in Vienna?"

"Budapest. Yes. She was a student of literature. She was never a professor, but she said she was. She came from money, she spoke half a dozen languages. Why did she marry my father? He was handsome, he looked like a success. But he was a disappointment. He became her exile. She came over just before the war. Her family was mostly lost in the camps. He was . . . a handsome disappointment. Now I don't see things the same way, I see him as some kind of broken hero, because every damned day, Peter, six days a week, you understand, he put on his pants, went down on the subway and sold his heart out for a bastard named Meyer, and brought home a paycheck that kept us going."

I can feel it wanting to spill out, and I take Peter's arm and change the subject to tonight's musical comedy as we walk back toward the corner, toward the ornate apartment building in yellow stone that served as one more pretext for my mother's bitterness. My mother and I would walk past on the way home and she'd sigh, "You see? *That's* where we should be living." But in the last years, when I was eleven, twelve, thirteen, before she went silent, what *didn't* serve as an image of her condition?

Now, father and son, we walk past those ghosts, mother and son, on our way to the subway. And in the roar of the train coming into the station, rumble and grinding down as we go from station to station, Eighty-sixth to Columbus Circle, I discover I want to say something over the noise, as if, as if if I don't, something between us, Peter and me, will be lost. And I'm amazed. I realize I've been holding my breath; now my breath comes deep,

like when you make love. Am I really going to do this? I find myself in panic, rehearsing phrases, phrases that begin sentences I
can't imagine myself saying.

We walk Central Park South to the St. Moritz, where we're
staying, and glancing over at the tape recorder in his hand to
make sure it's off, I say, "All right. You want to know about your
grandparents."

"I don't mean to push you, Dad. I know it's not your thing."

"It's okay. Well, my old man was a hardworking, old-
fashioned guy. Not very smart, Peter. I've told you that. Not
smart. He was crude. He used to brag that as a young man he and
a buddy would pick up 'faggots' just to beat them up. But at par-
ties he wore lamp shades on his head—you know what I mean?
He played handball and stayed away from home as much as he
could. My dad hated everybody in *categories*—not just 'faggots,'
'pansies, 'mamas' boys'—I was a 'mama's boy'—but 'wops,'
'micks,' 'chinks,' 'spics,' 'coons'—even 'kikes.' But with individu-
als, it was different. He was kind to the men at work—Cadillac
pushers they called them—black, Hispanic, guys who rolled
those huge racks of clothes around the street. Really kind. They
liked him. I could see it. Then he'd talk like that. So . . . I hated
him a lot. . . . He smacked me around. But he meant well. God, he
was like a big bear trapped in a zoo instead of off in a woods
somewhere."

"He hit you?"

"Ahh, not much. . . . People make such a big deal out of hitting. Hitting's no good, but that was the least of it. Anyway, that's
not what I want to tell you." I glance over at his tape recorder
again. He sees me, and he puts it in his book bag. "It's about your
grandmother. She suffered a lot. See, she was supposed to have a
different life. She'd wander through the house muttering to herself in languages I didn't understand. So she made *him* suffer.
When it got too bad, and she couldn't express any other way how

terrible, she used to get on her bony knees and stick her head in the oven and turn on the gas."

"She did? She did that?"

"Imagine—a parent doing a thing like that? Dramatizing her suffering like that in front of her child?"

" 'Her *child*'? Dad. You make it sound like it's somebody else."

"You see, Peter . . . Christ . . . see, I'm as old now as she was then. How long do I have to hold onto it all? You've got to let it go, eventually. There's nobody to complain to. How long can you keep a chip on your shoulder against the dead? And she could be so funny and charming. . . . "

"But it must have been so awful."

"She would have loved you. She would have been so proud. My mother. She'd put on a formal dress she hardly ever got the chance to really wear, she'd sit on top of the rented piano, ciga-rette dangling, legs crossed, and sing to me in a breathy German or French. Café songs. I loved it. Only a long time later I under-stood she was playing Lotte Lenya or Edith Piaf. . . .

"Well, as I say, partly it was drama. She was always telling the poor guy she was going to leave him. And he'd roar and shove her through the apartment, and this would justify her vision of her life, 'Go back to Europe, you crazy woman, maybe Hitler would take you back.' This was after the war, you understand, there was no Hitler. But there *had been* Hitler; so her eyes would roll up in her head, she'd maybe go into a faint or she'd rush to the medicine cabinet—'Say—which bottle do you think will do the job best?' "

"And then she died of a heart attack."

"Not exactly. . . . I know that's what I told you. No."

Peter waits for more. We pass the pompous architecture of the exclusive New York Athletic Club. More like a palazzo or a bank. No Jews, my mother used to tell me whenever we passed. No Jews.

Horse-drawn hansoms wait at the curb and carry lovers and families amid the taxis.

"Actually, honey, actually, she killed herself, your grandmother. When I was fourteen. That's what Sylvia was talking about before. Your mom never told you, did she?"

"Dad, how awful." I say nothing; I nod. "Dad? You never, never told me."

"No."

I hear his silence, and it makes me want to smooth things over. He doesn't ask and I don't say: *how.* I pick up the pace, I tell him I've always loved Central Park South. I tell him about Fitzgerald splashing in the fountain in front of the Plaza. Glory Town, Promise Town. "Peter, we're going to do New York up and down tonight. We'll have a snack before the show, but after, we'll take a cab down to Windows on the World and have a spectacular goddamn supper up on top and look out at all the lights."

And we do everything I wanted us to do, and the show is Gershwin and the taxi driver is a flamboyant Lebanese who used to be a trapeze artist, and we get the table I've reserved, at a window, and from a hundred-something stories up, New York looks like the promise of glory I used to think I wanted. But Peter is quiet. He keeps looking me over whenever I'm looking away. It isn't until the taxi ride home he says anything—then it's to ask what's wrong.

"With *me*, Peter? Wrong with *me*?"

"I guess it was telling me—I guess that's it? You've been so different. I don't think of you as ever heavy and sad like this. It's like you're somebody else."

"Oh, honey."

"No. I'm not stupid. I know you get sad, everybody gets sad."

"I didn't know it showed. I don't want it to spoil our weekend."

He looks at me so seriously, so *new*, that my mind falls into a gap; for half an instant I don't know this young man across the table. "Dad, it's all right. You got to be sad thinking about something like that. Your mother."

"Funny—and I thought *you* were the one feeling bad."

"Well, maybe. I guess. Maybe. I mean, it's so weird," he says. "Like all of a sudden you told me I was adopted or something."

"This isn't about *you,* honey."

He stares out of the cab. "It *is.* Sure it is."

"I guess it is. Well? You were the one wanted family history."

"Sure. *History.*"

"What do you mean, 'history' like that?"

"People are crazy," he says. "They hurt each other. That's family history. That's you and Mom. That's my history."

"I'm sorry I told you. I'm really sorry."

"*No.* You should have told me before this. How could you not tell me?"

"You think *I'm* crazy, too?"

We sleep late—or Peter sleeps late and I go down to the hotel gym and work out. I saw my father's face in dreams last night, first time in years. But in my dream it was a handsome face, not thick, bulbous-nosed. It was the face she must have loved once. I see it again as I jog the treadmill. It's almost half-past eleven by the time we get to Sylvia's. Riverside in the Eighties, high up over the river, a big, bright apartment just a couple of blocks from where she grew up.

The three women fuss over us a little, and I can see from the foyer the dining room table set with white linen and crystal. It makes me glad. Today, especially, I need all the formality I can get to enter any kind of dance.

Peter's brow is furrowed; I want to touch my fingers to his forehead.

Ruth and Alicia go off for coffee and come back carrying silver trays. The apartment is decorated to my soul's taste, in books and sunlight through plants and a hodgepodge of mahogany from any-old time. The Sunday *Times* is piled in sections by the old couch draped with a Turkish kilim. I feel at home with Ruth. She's a doctor, in family practice for an HMO, she's soft, a little heavy, comfortable in her body but firm in her carriage. She doesn't look at all like long, blonde Alicia. Things amuse Ruth; she holds them up for inspection: the muddle of their books by every chair, the talk of the young people about SATs and college applications.

We have coffee, and Sylvia goes off, comes back with a large black leather album embossed in gold. "This is what I wanted to show you." She pats the couch; Peter sits on one side, I on the other. "Look." She turns past pictures of her childhood, her father as I remember him, except that then he seemed old, now young. Her generous mother, who for a time, afterward, became *my* mother. And then I see myself in black and white, maybe twelve, thirteen, a handsome kid, a little pudgy, no teenaged acne yet, mouth twisted up in tough-guy irony at the camera, and next to me, Sylvia smiling full-face. We're in front of her old apartment house on West End.

"Look, Peter, you see?" I say, though what it is I want him to see I'm not sure. We turn the book around for Ruth and Alicia.

Sylvia turns the page. "*This* one," she says. Sylvia as a young girl, maybe thirteen, wearing a flowered dress, so pretty, her hair long and dark, my parents behind her. I must have taken that one. Vaguely, I remember there were times our parents got together. The next picture is in a park. My mother's all dolled up, she's wearing a broad summer hat, pale linen I think, and a silk dress—I remember the dress, navy blue, silk—perhaps she was trying to impress Sylvia's parents.

But Sylvia sighs, "She was always so stylish, your mother. Do you remember that? And look at that hand on her hip. The *grande dame.*"

Peter's bent over the photograph so I can't see. "Sorry," he says, sitting back. "That's practically the first picture of your mother I've seen. Except for her wedding picture. You know that, Dad?"

"Stylish . . . " I say. "Look, Syl, look at how false. You and I look like boyfriend and girlfriend here, and they—they look *happy.* Now, I'm sorry, but that's simply not the way it was. My mother?—I told Peter last night," I say, "about my mother's death." I announce this to all of them, as if assuming they've talked about it among themselves, and I see I'm right—there's no surprise. I catch irritation in my voice—as if Sylvia had forced me to tell Peter. As if she had intruded, as if she had a long history of intruding. "No, not so happy."

"I know," she says. "But *look* at her. How proud of you . . . "

I see what she means. My mother's putting on an act, of course, smiling, face tilted to be charming, but she's got a hand on my shoulder, in possession and pride, I see the look Sylvia means. And instantly I feel heavy, I catch the scent of her powder, I feel smothered. "Well, you're getting a history lesson," I tell Peter. "About the unreliability of photographs."

"Maybe they *were* happy that afternoon," he says quietly, as if it were simply one logical possibility. I hear annoyance.

"I do think so," Sylvia says. "You know, I liked your mother. She was very loving to me."

I don't say anything. I wish we could leave. I look out at the Hudson, that grayest river. Ruth finds a crack on the ceiling to stare at. Alicia and Peter avoid each other's eyes. Peter's been staring at me whenever I look elsewhere. The brunch about to be served feels like an ordeal.

Now one more photograph, this one in color, the color fading.

"This must have been a different afternoon," she says. "She's wearing the same dress but look, there, there's our Mr. Ornstein at the picnic table. You remember?"

I shrug. "No."

"You *don't remember?* He played violin those Thursday nights?"

"No."

"Your mother was very fond of him. *Daniel.* You don't remember?"

"*No,* I don't remember. There must have been a violinist, but I don't remember." *What do you want of me?* The man is in a dark suit. He looks seedy but interesting. His face is long, handsome, hawklike. He has heavy, black eyebrows. It comes back a little. "I don't remember him exactly, but I think I remember his face." I look more closely at the picture. My mother and father, Sylvia's mother and father, are posing by a tree. The man is seated, he just happens to be in the picture. He's smiling up at them.

"Maybe *I* remember so well," Sylvia says, "because we used to gossip about it. My mother and my father." She glances at Peter, and seeing the look, I puff out my lips, give a toss of my hand, as if to say, *Go on, say what you want—what can it matter?*

"There's nothing to tell."

"She liked him?" I prompt.

"Well, yes. *Yes.* He was a man of culture. A scholar, a musician. He taught at N.Y.U. He spoke I don't know how many languages. She began coming over on Thursday nights to see him—that's how it was that *you* came at first. They spoke German for hours. Your father . . . didn't like him."

"I bet. I'll bet he called him a 'goddamn refugee.'"

"But *you* did—you liked him very much."

"*Ornstein.*"

"That's right."

I go inside the picture. Ornstein. Now, saying the name, I feel his long hands, long fingers. I remember his heavy breath, or imagine that I do. I look at him looking at her. He wanted to marry her, I wanted him to marry her? . . . Am I making that up? I don't know. This memory, the sense of their relationship, holds together like the skin of a bubble, as if, were I to breathe, it would dissolve.

Sylvia says, "My father worried your father felt humiliated."

"You remember one hell of a lot," I say, and Ruth looks over at me; I know she's hearing something in my tone. She nods to Alicia, they go off to set the food on the table. From the kitchen, Alicia calls, "Peter? Will you give us a hand?"

He excuses himself. He doesn't meet my eyes. I close the album and sit back, shading my eyes from the bright day outside, my stomach turning over.

"Remember a lot?" Sylvia repeats, very serious. "I suppose I do. Maybe that's why you stopped returning my calls, stopped writing. Was I too nosy?"

"You went away to college. That's all. Kids lose touch."

"I was home on vacations."

"Who knows after all this time?"

"Your mother stopped coming over," Sylvia says, "after Mr. Ornstein went to the West Coast. And wasn't it just a few weeks later . . . "

"So that was your family's story?"

"Yes."

"I have a different view—I can't remember a time she didn't talk about doing it." I say this flatly, authoritatively, a little bitterly.

"I'm sure we romanticized the situation. I don't mean to argue with you, Daniel. It doesn't matter."

"Maybe it was a catalyst. Ornstein leaving her. I didn't even remember that this Ornstein left, but *maybe*. We never put that together. . . . Or maybe my father did. Who knows after all this time? . . . Sylvia, you're still upset with me, aren't you? That I disappeared. You're getting back at me!"

"You know, I suppose I really am." She laughs as if she's surprised. "It's odd, Daniel. It's been bothering me a little all these years. . . . "

I find something funny in this. I take her hand in my two hands. "I'm sorry."

She encloses my hands. "It's so long ago."

We're called in to the dining room, and we spread great, starched white napkins, and Ruth sighs, "We do love Sundays. We stitch ourselves together into human beings every Sunday morning."

A Schubert trio is playing. I can't help thinking of my mother: how she would have loved to be here; but how she would have lost everything—the smell of good breads and the music, and the young people, Peter and Alicia, and Ruth and Sylvia—by trying to establish herself as The Duchess, by experiencing this Sunday grace merely as what was lacking in her own life.

We talk about larger sadnesses. Children who grow up without nourishment of body and soul. The way hope seems to be closing down in America. A meanness that first degrades, then blames and punishes those who are degraded. Like something out of Dickens. Oddly, as we speak of these things, my stomach calms, I rest in our shared sadness.

I think this larger pain is seductive. I think I need its music in order to permit myself to feel my own sorrows—but put them in perspective. Our collective sorrow—feeling it, speaking of it this way—is like a penance for self-indulgence. It comforts.

Only for a while. As I drift down into the griefs we share, I find my breath heavy and damp, and I see a hotel room not a mile away, cheap hotel, respectable, no flophouse but not the Ritz, God knows. God knows, no place for a duchess. I turn away to other music, the Schubert trio this Sunday morning floats upon, and I snatch a piece of smoked white fish, my first in years. Now something in the music or in this food, European-Jewish, something in the bookcases full of new and ragged books, something in the dark woods and crystal in an old glass-fronted breakfront I seem to remember from Sylvia's old apartment, something brings me a word: *foreigner,* I hear it in my father's voice, not *refugee* but *foreigner,* and all at once I *see* Mr. Ornstein and I think, *Oh, Mr. Ornstein, that Mr. Ornstein . . .* and of *course* I know Ornstein, and now I see him by the oval sailboat pond in Central Park near Fifth Avenue, I see him pushing off his handmade schooner with a pole tipped like a cane, with rubber.

They're talking, Sylvia and Ruth, about public indifference to children. Peter tells them, "My history teacher says, 'We reap what we sow.' But the thing is, *we* reap what *they* sow. I'm not the one who's indifferent. But I'm going to be the victim of their indifference." I've never heard Peter speak like this. The Peter I knew was a child.

Sylvia fills our cups with coffee, and touching my forehead I say, "Sylvia—I just remembered: Ornstein made a beautiful wooden sailboat; not just a sloop—a schooner. It was his weekend hobby. It was all fitted with brass cleats and winches and white sails. The hull glowed under layers and layers of shellac. Did you ever see it?"

"I don't think so."

"Funny!—now that I can see *it,* I can see *him.*" I stop. *Goddamn foreigner,* I hear in my father's voice. Am I inventing? I don't know. "He *gave* me that boat," I say.

"When he left New York?"

"I don't know. Maybe. We used to sail it together, I remember that, I remember the three of us going often to the little pond, he rented a berth for it—you know that brick building by the pond?"

"You and your mother and Ornstein."

"And he *gave* it to me. Where is Ornstein now? Is he still alive?"

"Oh, Daniel, I don't know. We lost touch."

I nod and stay silent and talk drifts away, I take part, oh, but I'm not here now. Alicia and Peter are talking about their futures. I'm remembering my mother and Mr. Ornstein. I remember them sitting on a park bench together by the pond, I remember how proud I was to borrow his pole and sail his boat for him. And I'm wondering—that boat, what could have happened to that beautiful boat? He *gave* it to me, I'm sure of that, and it was precious, I would never have gotten rid of it—then what?

While the others are still lazing over brunch, I go look out the window—it's not polite, but I do—and I watch a big cabin cruiser making a V-wake down the Hudson, and I watch the Sunday traffic heading out of the city for family Sundays and I remember family Sundays, the silent drives, and Sylvia stands next to me and touches my arm, and I realize I've been waiting for her.

"You came to the funeral," I say.

"Of course."

"I can't remember much. Can you?"

"No. I remember you."

"They didn't want me to see her, but I did." There's a velvet cushion on the radiator; we both sit there and stare out at the river. Laughter from the dining room. I look into Sylvia's face. "You know, I guess by the time I got to Columbia, I wanted to be somebody else, not that boy you felt sorry for. I suppose that's it. Why I stopped calling."

"I think so, Daniel."

" . . . Finally, she looked like a duchess. Lying there in blue silk. I was afraid I was going to laugh and they'd send me to a psychiatrist."

"But you handled things. I mean—not perfectly, but well."

"I did. I made my accommodations."

Now we don't say a lot of things for a long minute. But it feels comfortable. "Isn't Ruth wonderful?" she says, finally. She kisses my cheek. "You'll come back and see us?" I take her hand, we walk back to the others.

We have a couple of hours before the train to Boston. "There's a place I need to see, okay?" I ask. "Please. For me. It's just a few blocks away."

Peter shrugs, he humors me, but I feel he's walking by himself. We walk from Riverside over to Amsterdam, up Amsterdam and down a side street to a refurbished hotel on the corner of

Columbus, flat gray stone, with new steel-banded windows. I
haven't been here for thirty years. At first, I went out of my way to
come by after school—maybe to see if I could. Then, never.

There used to be wood-cased sash windows, the hotel name
engraved in the glass door was different, and the glass, I remember, was cracked diagonally, corner to corner on the door. "This
is the place. . . . My mother walked out one night, I don't know
why, I mean why *then*—a fight, I suppose."

"Maybe this man she liked?"

"That's what Sylvia thinks. I don't know. She took her fancy
suitcase. She had this one Louis Vuiton case from Europe. With
fleur-de-lis. . . . We called all over the city, but my father and I
were imagining the Plaza, the Pierre—high drama, you know?
Instead, she came here, I don't know, because it was nearby, because, maybe, it expressed her spirit that day? I don't know. Or
maybe because of the gas. Those days, residential hotels, some of
them, still had gas. I think she figured on that."

"So that's how she killed herself?"

"No. No, I think that's what she imagined, you see? *Gas.* But
no. This place had electric kitchens. No. I'm simply guessing she
imagined . . . because she used to talk all the time about gas."

It takes him three or four breaths to ask. "Then—what,
Dad?"

"Oh . . . well, she used a razor blade." I stop.

It's night in my mind. Ambulance and a cop car, whirling red
lights. I don't speak about this. My father driving around the
neighborhood, hunting, when the call came. I don't tell Peter it
was me, I was the one got the call and left him a note and came
down here. Columbus Avenue in the night.

And a police lieutenant didn't want to let me up, but I started
screaming at him, I acted crazy beyond what I was feeling, I
watched myself doing it, crazy for effect, or so I thought, and he
gave in and put an arm around my shoulder and took me up. He
had whiskey on his breath, he needed deodorant. I can feel his

hand around my shoulder, I wanted to make a gesture of shrugging it off but I was afraid he'd really take his hand away, and he was all I had.

They'd cleaned up the worst of it, she was lying on a rubber sheet, there was still blood, blood on the floor, handprints of blood on the wallpaper, and the room stank of cigarettes and everything else. There was a bottle of sherry; it was more than half full.

I said, *That's my mother,* the way it was said in the movies. Deadpan. I *felt* deadpan. I think I wanted to make some kind of theatrical display equal to the situation, but I couldn't. The room was bare, the bed was covered in what looked like a brown army blanket. The shade was up. I could see the throbbing red light of the police cruiser, I could see Columbus Avenue. I think now she condemned herself to a prison to carry out sentence.

My father came and took me home.

Suddenly, *I know what happened to the boat.* What must have happened: my father. I don't know exactly, but I understand. And I understand that in the turmoil, I decided to pretend to forget about the boat until, after a while, I really couldn't remember.

We walk down Columbus toward Eighty-first. Across the street, the old saloon, plate-glass windows still framed in heavy, dark, shellacked wood, where the man with the bloody face got tossed out into the gutter.

Peter says: "Dad? Are you all right, Dad? You want to go somewhere and sit down?"

I stop on the street. My hands are cupped, held up to Peter as if they contained the story. "She went out *without stockings.* I don't think she ever in her whole life . . . I think she was playing Ophelia—remember?—the mad scene from *Hamlet?* You know . . . maybe I *would* like to sit down, Peter."

Peter's hand is planted on my back all the way to a bench on Central Park West. I let it stay. "Afterward, she was less absent in the house than before; she was always there."

He's frowning in sympathy; I feel cheap for requiring sympathy. I touch the knot between his eyes with my forefinger, and he smiles with irony at my solicitude. But what I'm feeling isn't just solicitude. It's shame. This isn't the father I want to be. I've been the adventurer father. Now I feel my own sad father filling my living bones.

You want family history? Here's family history. My father coming home like a rag and slumping by the stove, cooking hamburgers and home fries, night after night, with canned peas, rye bread from the bakery at the corner, or—when he was just too wiped out—taking me to the deli, roast beef for me, liverwurst for himself because it was cheap. Smell of brine from the pickle barrel. Smell of my father's sweat and dirt after a day dragging samples store to store. Walking home along Columbus after dark, he didn't talk. Sometimes he patted my shoulder—a beat and two half-beats over and over. He had a big belly, his "corporation." It was an effort to carry it home. Still, usually he'd poke me and grin as if he were suggesting an illicit drug—we'd stop for ice cream. Then he'd fall asleep in the big chair, newspaper over his belly. I'd do my homework. And my mother wouldn't prowl, cigarette in hand, in her old blue housecoat. She wouldn't light *Yortzeit* candles for her family that didn't get away from Hitler. She no longer sat on the toilet gazing into inner space, tapping the ashes from her cigarette between her legs.

I sit on the bench by Central Park patting my son's shoulder. A beat and two half-beats, over and over. "My father needed . . . reassurance. Now she was gone, he wasn't so angry, he didn't need me as something for them to quarrel about. He needed me to keep him getting up in the morning, going down in the subway to his job. I said he was a kind of hero? See, he kept doing his job, coming home and cooking terrible dinners. My aunt came from Los Angeles, she offered to take me off his hands. He said *no*. You see?"

There's a filthy, chemical cloud soaked in sun just starting to set over Jersey. It's gorgeous—I want him to feel how splendid so *I* can feel it. I want to borrow Being. I want Peter's smile to dissipate what's going on in my heart. I point at the sky, Peter nods, uninterested. He looks serious, looks sad. Backlit by the late sun he himself glows but he doesn't know it.

"She didn't mean to leave me—but she left," I say. "And he didn't want to stay—but he stayed." Now, as I say this—say it to put it away in my pocket with an encapsulating irony—a silence brews underneath the city music. There's no beauty in this silence. Into the silence something thick and grim and dark seeps, and I'm dizzy and can hardly breathe; for an instant I wonder am I having a heart attack? But it's not that—it's what we're neither of us saying. I say it: "Yes. All right. My father stayed, at least he stayed."

Peter looks at me with the new intense look. "You left."

I sit with this. It takes me time to look at him. "I knew you were thinking that. It's not completely fair. I drove hours on weekends to see you. Didn't I? I *had* to leave for my work, I mean Brattleboro, what kind of place for a business consultant was that?"

He doesn't argue.

"Yes. All right, I know there's more, Peter."

He looks away, at the cars and buses that pass on Central Park West.

"I know. The truth is, your mother and I, when we separated, I wanted to be anywhere else. So I went to Boston. I'm sorry, Peter. I am sorry."

" 'Sorry' won't cut it. You left. You *did* leave. I never said anything. Did I? I never did. But I guess 'Sorry' won't cut it."

He says this gently, and that makes it worse. "No, it won't. I left. I did leave you. And I know what that feels like, don't I?"

"Oh, I know there's no com*par*ison, Dad." But he says this as if he's angry that it's true.

"I know there *is*," I say.

Now the silence we share grows different; strange; not angry, not peaceful. Oh, there's no radiance, forget about radiance. But it's become something we *do* share, Peter and I, this silence, full of grief, but *ours*—a third party on this park bench. Some of it is purely my own, I know that. I'm the only one sees my mother so ashamed of her life she punishes herself by walking around the house all day in the same housedress streaked with sour cream, her face ravaged, the pencilled lines of her eyebrows blurred; and the ash gets so long at the end of her cigarette I wait with a hollow in my stomach for it to crumple into the bowl. The hollow is still there; that's mine. And the fact that it's mine means that Peter can never know what I know, as I can never know what he's gone through.

But in a way this gap is what we share. We sit with it as the families pass by on their way to or from the park, kids rushing ahead, we nurse it between us like our sick child, and once in a while Peter looks at me or I lift my eyebrows like a gesture in some code I don't know how to translate, until it's almost too late to pick up our things at the hotel and catch the train for Boston.

# Glory

*This* is a story about glory, not mourning, but there'd be no story to tell if Avrom Hirsch didn't lose his best friend, his only close friend, to cancer. Cancer of the everything. Slow, so slow it seems he can barely remember the time before (though it was less than a year), and Avrom lives in terror for Ben, terror of the pain, as he's always feared pain for himself, so it's not just in sympathy but in shame, as if it's Avrom's own physical cowardice that made life choose Ben for the torture.

But the pain is kept down. What happens instead is that over the next six, eight months, more and more of Ben Seigelman's life is closed off. Now he can't walk fast, now can't walk at all. He sits; now he can't sit; he's propped up in bed, and now he has to lie down. He can't write anymore, but he can read, and knowing he's likely to die, he takes to the books that meant the most to him—*Middlemarch, The Tempest*, the stories of Chekhov, and the poetry of Williams and Yeats and Blake. Ben is a computer scientist, but he studied literature at Reed, and it's always been his passion. Sunday mornings, Avrom and Ben used to go out for bagels, and the two families would brunch together, and afterward, the men would take a walk and often talk about what they were reading. So now, afternoons, Avrom stops over after work to sit by Ben's bedside and read aloud. Until one day Ben shakes his head.

"Ave, the thing is . . . " (and then a pause; the pauses get longer week by week) " . . . when you read me a page or when I read a page, it's as clear to me as it ever was, but the page before, I can't remember. . . . God is finally making me live in the fucking present," he says, and they both laugh. "And how do you follow a novel in the present?" Ben's head floats slowly from side to side in the sea of his cancer. "In a sense, it's a gift. I can read everything I love over and over again like it's the first time."

"Maybe we better stick to poetry," Avrom says.

And now even the poetry won't go down, and he sits, taking turns with Ben's wife, Susan, holding his friend's hand sometimes for a half hour, and sometimes Ben is awake and sometimes he sleeps, and at night Avrom listens for a call. He even wants the call to come.

Sometimes Kristin visits with Avrom, but more often she leaves Ben to him. It's unusual for a professional actress, but she's always been reserved. Avrom has stopped fighting her about that, stopped demanding that she be expressive. Now her calm, distant grace helps him. She soothes by not soothing too much. Micah soothes by being five years old. At night, so much the best time, leaning over the boy's bed, Avrom kisses him in the middle of his warmth, his special blanket and special bear—the eyes of the others, wolf and rabbit, watching over; five years old—kisses Micah's cheek, or not exactly kisses but rather keeps lips pressed to his cheek and breathes more deeply than he's breathed all day; warmth and smell of him almost erotic but that's not it, Avrom considers, it's the other way around; exactly: that sometimes, making love, Kristin and I can get to this sweetness. Avrom looks up the prayer in the siddur. He prays for Micah and Kristin when he prays for Ben. *May the Holy One, blessed be God, remove from them all sickness, preserve them in health . . .*

Micah, their small hostage to life: Avrom pictures, when he says the name, not Micah the prophet but flakes of shining stone. But soft. Skin so delicate, and all the mystery of the soft parts inside that have to work just right. I want to keep him like this, this long burrowing into his cheek.

And when the call comes, Avrom lets go and again his breath comes deep, and when he is through, he goes to sit with Susan until Ben's sons get to Boston from Seattle, from Sante Fe. Then all the next night he sits shiva with the sons, Steve and Charlie, sits all night with the body of his friend. The younger son, Steve, a practicing Jew, wrapped in his prayer shawl, is the one to say the prayers for the dead. Mostly they three sit in silence, and Avrom keeps thinking, *Nothing will ever be the same.*

When he met Ben, they were in their late twenties, 1970, in a political "affinity group" in Boston. But they became friends one night when, stoned, they admitted that political analysis bored the shit out of them, that sure, the war had to be resisted, but really they preferred Groucho to Karl, as they preferred Brahms to the Stones, George Eliot to Situationist manifestos.

Ben was the friend Avrom took long walks with, all these years walked the Esplanade by the Charles across from M.I.T., where Ben taught, skaters passing, sailboats and sculls on the river, and talked about computers and business or, much more, about the new America of deep-structure poverty. Or they agreed to read the same stories by Chekhov or the novels of Nabokov. And they talked about God; not about God's existence—Ben liked to say that was a bullshit question—but about God's presence in a passage of Torah. Even with God Ben was tough. Ben had to be the hard-nosed guy; it was the only way he could talk about God—if he kept the talk tough. But they could both talk about the gap between words and the pulse of life, and agreed that the gap was not necessarily an empty place, might in fact be a place of fullness, the place where God hung out, while all words could ever do was point. The gap between God and the language was one thing; the other was the gap between this world—which both of them took for granted was a broken one—and our longings for God.

Ben hung out on one side of the gap—the world was broken, filled with evil—and Avrom on the other. Their friendship sometimes felt—Ave said this once, and then they kept silence for many minutes, peculiar in two talkative Jews—a memorial to the world it might have been.

When Avrom Hirsch loses Ben Seigelman it is as if the hollow place under the words has grown bigger. He feels pregnant with emptiness. He speaks at the memorial service at M.I.T., makes sure Susan comes to brunch on Sunday and the next Sunday. Avrom fantasizes asking her to move in with them—as if he were some desert patriarch. And Susan, Susan has her work, she's a psychologist, she has her friends—Kristin for one, though she and Susan have never been as close as he and Ben. And she has the boys.

First thing in the morning, when Avrom gets to the office, he turns on his computer and checks his e-mail; every day he has the same fantasy—of seeing on his screen a message from Ben. Well, it's because Ben is so mixed in his mind with computers. Avrom imagines, wills himself to imagine, that in the billions of chips out there are remnants of Ben's consciousness, the synapses of a soul. One morning he closes his eyes to think a Ben that might be reconfigured out of all the connections among those points. Right away he stands up and closes down the machine, furious at himself. You phony bastard! Sugar! Bullshit! Uch! Listen—if all the remnants were recombined so you could store them on a single hard drive, there'd be nothing of Ben.

There are times he forgets and thinks of calling Ben. It's still that way since his mother died last summer. *Mom will appreciate that. . . . Is that crazy? That's not so crazy.*

The school bus that hit an antitank mine is gutted, stripped to twisted black steel; paper is caught by the wind; scraps of clothing, hardly colored at all, as if all the color has been blown away, cling to a twisted chain-link fence and, as the camera pans, to branches of a burned tree. The bodies are gone but men and women in dark clothing hover over the ground like birds looking for food.

In China thousands are executed every year. Their organs are harvested for transplants. Connect these two sentences.

The soldier who forced a Bosnian next-door neighbor to drink his grandchild's blood. A mother whose . . . a father whose . . .

And so on.

*You've got to talk to me, Ave. You have a responsibility to talk. . . .* And then

*You have a child. I don't care about me so much. You've got to talk. . . . And then*

*It's not the end of the world, Ave.*

For a week the ground, whatever floor he stands on, has been tilting, and a high sound half hum, half siren, faint, faraway, comes closer.

Four young men in California, worshipers of Satan, tortured and raped and murdered a sixteen-year-old virgin in order to win entrance to hell.

A man is arraigned in superior court for manslaughter. He was sodomizing his girlfriend's five-year-old daughter; to keep her from screaming he pressed her face into a pillow.

The Charles River bends and bends again toward Boston Harbor. Ducks and sculls on the steel-gray river. Sometimes

Avrom talks to himself; more often he is silent in his head. He wishes he had something to say. He wishes Ben were there to face things so terrible. He wishes he were a Jew, really a Jew, like his grandfather, so he could sit in temple and say Kaddish.

Before the river opens and the sky, before the world breaks apart like a pomegranate to reveal its seeds, he hears cries of gulls, car alarms, drone or whine of planes, fragments of a bewildering music. He listens; it's only noise.

When the sky opens, he's biking the Esplanade, looking across the river. Or rather he's stopped, he's leaned his bike against a tree. He wraps his arms around himself and rocks, as if he wore a prayer shawl, like old men davening in temple. He rocks.

And now the sky opens; or is it the air? But that's not it, because the gray river opens as well, and the buildings of Boston University, and downtown, and the grass of early spring and the sounds that were only noise. *Opens.* And his chest, and so the hollowness is exposed to, is contiguous to, the new openness, which rushes in to fill him.

He is aware of the air opening in the middle of the air. It's like one of those pictures that look like a two-dimensional pattern of colored shapes, but if you stare long enough you see the fragments receding and others coming forward and it's a lion or dragon in three dimensions, and everything you saw before is still there but now it's part of a different picture.

For there's nothing new. He's seeing, Avrom is seeing, the ordinary world, or not "seeing" so much as being sewn with threads of light into the world, fibre by fibre. But it's nothing like LSD, which he remembers well, there are no flashings and color bleeds, nor is it like being stoned—the *opposite!*—for when he was stoned, things vibrated with such intensity because the frames and edges were dulled, so there was nothing but the one experience, *the loaf of bread on the table,* but now, when the air opens, he sees everything underneath and behind and on all sides, sees in more and more context. The contexts are multiplied and seem to exist in time as well as space.

And seeing, he can step inside, his spiritual metabolism has speeded up, like a fly in human time; can slow up the film so that the fly moves in human time and the human hand trying to catch it lumbers, slow as an elephant.

Take that Back Bay house, black fire escape facing the river: the umber stone wall "opens." What does "open" mean? The wall takes on depth, it pulses with its own being, exists not just in space but in time. He can see it inside its time, it vibrates with its existence in time so that Avrom is aware of the workers who laid the brick and stone in the late nineteenth century after Back Bay was filled and streets formed, and is aware of pain behind the wall, not its precise nature but certainly pain. It doesn't seem a projection of his own pain.

Even the atomic structure that makes up the universe is only the temporary shape of something, the form it happens on, no more or less real than a hologram. Bach understood this; and the place between the notes is an indication, a guide.

In slight panic, giddy, he holds the railing of the Esplanade and reassures himself. Oh, the world is out there; it simply isn't what he'd believed it to be. In a song any note is what it is only because you know what went before and what will come after. Without memory and expectation there is no music. He remembers Ben saying you can't read a novel in the pure present. It's the same with all existence. This fragile version of world takes its significance, its being, from context, from time and, oh, my God, so many other relations, so that each thing in itself is webbed into a mesh of things, times, people. He was here, walking last year, with Ben. He was here last week with Micah. They're still here, part of things now. Each thing, leaf, tree, house, moment of shimmering river, is a temporary, insanely complex poem that speaks itself in relation to a thousand things inside silence and time.

He is aware now that he is crazy; so perhaps he is not in fact crazy. He is simply aware of the lines of connection. *If I were aware of more, how could I deal with it?* He is sure that there *is* more.

He carries his bike over the footbridge above Storrow Drive, and as he bikes slowly along Commonwealth, he could say he sees ghosts walking on each side of people.

He's from a family of atheists, Jews who were no Jews, though he was named Avrom in honor of his grandfather, who died somewhere in Poland during the war, in a camp or in Warsaw— they heard both stories. He has tried only lately to be a Jew, and then in a clumsy way. He's ashamed he can't even read Hebrew decently; only recently, his finger pointing out the words as if he were six years old again, has he begun to read the prayers in Hebrew. He's studied very little, he's prayed very little. He has no preparation, why should this come to him? But, then, what does the opening of the world into fuller being—what does it have to do with God? Maybe nothing. It's just what is.

(

Kristin has seen him lately burrowing into himself, squirreling himself away from her, worse and worse, for months now, even before Ben died. Friends call, he won't go out. She has taken to cooking seriously every night she's home; nights when she has rehearsals or student performances or a late meeting, she makes sure their sitter gets the table set with napkins in rings, candles, the curtains drawn against the dismal half-dark of early spring evenings. Indian food, Cajun, West African, Mexican—it dawns on her she's trying all the spicy foods she knows to try to wake his spirit, woo him back to this world. Friday nights, though not a Jew herself, Kristin coaxes Ave to say the Sabbath prayers. *You're not dying. It's not the end of the world. You have a child.*

But he *knows* he has a child. It's his one connection. He holds Micah too often, too tightly.

And this goes on. She, too, loved Ben, God knows. And since his death she talks to Susan once or twice a week. It's something she can't fully express, and it frustrates her, his brooding silence, as if Ave thinks he has a monopoly on grief. When he speaks he half whispers, so you have to say, *What? What, honey?* And then half the time he shrugs and won't say.

She wonders, should she call Harvard Health and make an appointment for him? For now tonight he's come home with a new walk. He's a tall, lanky man, gawky sometimes. It's endearing; she noticed it when they first met. She used to tease him with *Abe* or *Honest Abe* instead of Ave. It's odd, after living with a man for fifteen years, to find suddenly, tonight, his walk has changed: he plants / his feet / slowly, he plants *himself* in his red chair. Kristin teaches drama and theater at B.U.—she can't help reading the body, the stories it tells, but this story she doesn't understand. If he were a character in a Chekhov play, which would he be? She's tempted to think, he's in *slow motion*—but that's not it. It's as if tonight he were from another planet and not quite used to our atmosphere.

She sits across from him pretending to read the paper and watches. Worried—and yet, isn't there something strong, the way his arm rests on the arm of that chair? He isn't sad tonight. He's been so full of heavy sighs. *Oh, your gefilte-fish sighs,* she teases; his breath is thick and hot with them. Not tonight.

Micah's been picked up by Stephanie at kindergarten; only a few minutes till they're back. She wants to sit down next to him and touch his hair and say, *I know, I know.* But she can't. "Can I get you a drink? Micah's at the library."

No drink. He looks into her eyes the way he does when they're about to make love. He closes his eyes. "Ben's here," he says. He waves his hand toward the space between them.

*Now* she's worried. She goes off to the kitchen for a bottle of red wine and pours herself a glass. She asks him what he's seeing.

He looks into her face again and says, "I never understood. Now I understand." That's all. He waves his fingers as if touching or pointing. "I mean *about Ben*." And he goes to her, sits on the arm of her chair. "Poor honey, you poor honey."

She lets go; cries and cries without explanation, and he strokes her hair. "You had to keep it to yourself," he says. "You couldn't even mourn him decently, not the way you needed."

"No."

"No."


It was Ben who introduced her to Avrom. Kristin and Ben had been lovers on and off for a few years, since she studied drama at Yale and he'd been finishing his doctorate there. Kristin sees a borrowed graduate student apartment, sunny afternoon, movie posters covering cracks in the walls. They'd made love deliberately and tenderly, and now they were dressing as if it were so preoccupying to get dressed they couldn't spare the time to look at one another. Ben waited (so she supposes now) till they were protected by their clothes, and then he took her hand and sat down with her on the mattress that was the only furniture in that room.

"Love," he said, "love, I've met a real good guy. He's doing a degree in economics, but he's a good guy, he loves music, he can talk literature. He's becoming a friend. His name is Avrom Hirsch. I think I want to introduce you."

And she said, grieving, feeling herself like an astronaut cut off from a mother ship, floating nowhere, "So. Are you handing me over?"

"Look into my eyes, Kris. Does it look that way? Do you think I'm just 'handing you over'? Do you think? I've got my sons."

But of course he was handing her over. She's forgiven and not forgiven. Look what came out of it: Avrom, who became dear to her, then Micah.

For three years when she and Ave were first married, she kept apart from Ben except for dinners and walks as families. And then there was a weekend afternoon on the Vineyard when they found themselves alone. And then he called and said he couldn't be without her. Then six months later she was the one to call. And so on.

She burrows into Avrom's chest and he mothers her. Coming up for air, she asks, "What do you mean, you say Ben's here?"

"It's all right," he says.

"Then you knew about me and Ben?"

"I know now."

"It's not been for years, Ave. Not since Micah. *Before.*"

"I don't mean 'all right' like that. That, too, Kristin. But I mean that I think *Ben's* all right. I don't know for sure. But I think. I mean we don't have to worry."

She pulls back and looks at him. She's irritated by this other-worldly crap. What role is he performing? She wishes he'd just show he's hurt and angry, get it over with, so they can go on. Did he find an old letter? Did Ben tell him at the end? "How do you know? What do you mean 'seeing'?"

"I mean I see it. In my skin, as if my skin had eyes."

"Ave, stop. Please?"

"He's in this room, but not a ghost. It's good to have him, he's here for both of us. Well, this room is very full," he laughs. "I'm trying to get a handle."

☾

Avrom sits in the rose velvet old wing-backed chair trying out his new skin, naked to the air. His mother is present in all her caustic elegance, his father, dead fifteen years, in a heavy brooding anger; the living room is very full, full of living, of past lives not past. He takes Kristin's hand. He's told her, *Ben's all right.* Well, Ben *is.* Still—there's something dark and hurt about him.

The seeing doesn't go away. His mother smokes, cigarette between stiffened forefinger and middle finger. It's at the precise moment she has warned him not to marry a shikse. A Christian woman. *Oh,* she says, *I can see the attraction: that aristocratic insouciance of hers. But her lips are too thin, my dear.* Then: *Oh, don't mind me,* she says drily, playing masochist, but arch, parodic, so that she doesn't have to own the masochism, *if you want to put me in the grave, my dear, why it's perfectly all right. But you must know what they're like?* He remembers laughing, Mom, what about Joan of Arc? *Well, and didn't she dress up in men's clothes?*

When Avrom was a child, he used to lie in bed and stare at the frame of the window against city lights. He learned he could alter the window, make it grow small and smaller, till he became afraid each night that if he kept on it would become untenably small, smaller than he would be able to label a visual trick. And then where would *he* be, would he dissolve out of the shared world?

There are strings of attachment between himself and Ben, between Ben and Kristin. It's as if he could pluck them for their music. He wishes she could have told him—if she had, she could have grieved more completely. He thinks: *a triangle,* thinks it visually—a complete, stable figure—he feels his own point in the figure.

He's never been so full of her. Kristin nestles against him. And he takes comfort; after all, she's not naturally a nestler. If you cut your hand open on a shard of glass, as he did last month, and the wound poured blood, you'd want Kristin there to handle things, to bandage you while keeping Micah calm. She nestles. He wonders: who's comforting whom?

In the morning, it's gone. Avrom wakes to a house full of ordinary life. There's no depth in the air, no matter how he tries to see it, the window is open, it's spring, and there are car noises from Beacon Street, bird songs, but the air is closed, the world has flattened into the present; and no one's present but Kristin, who, still asleep, curls away from his waking. As usual, he thanks God for the morning in Hebrew words he has learned by rote. He looks around him wondering how he can coax the air to open again.

He does his stretches in Micah's room, humming, "Wake up, time to wake up, big boy." Micah wakes slowly, but once awake, he's singing. Loud child, gorgeous in his bravado, he sings, "Some day he'll come along, the man I love . . . " like a torch singer, quoting a style a decade gone when Avrom was a child. Look, he thinks, how we poke through the closet and choose an instrument of language, and the past issues through us.

Micah is especially sunny this morning, and Avrom sits in the good-night chair and watches him pick out his clothes; for a change he doesn't complain about his jeans or the way his belt feels. Kristin fixes breakfast; she doesn't talk about last night. She's teaching today; she's dressed in a soft wool skirt, heather, and a mauve blouse; years ago, he thinks, she wore only cool clothes, black and white, pants, and her hair, now trim but long, was cut like a boy's. He's known this change without knowing; now, when she's turned away, he stares.

He drives Micah to school in Cambridge, then down to his office around the corner from the State House.

He does what his grandfather did, and his grandfather's grandfather. He buys and he sells. His grandfather bought and sold sheep; Avrom buys and sells—internationally—containerloads of coffee, fruit, electronics, it doesn't matter. It hasn't changed much since the fourteenth century; a merchant fills a ship's hold with goods to sell, then takes on cargo for the return voyage. Avrom doesn't own the ship; he's not even the merchant. He finds space, he finds cargoes. Now it's telephone and fax, it's planes as much as ships, trucks as much as planes, and sometimes it's nothing for days, futile calls to arrange deals that fall through, deals that never had real backing. But sometimes he can spot a potential buy in Egypt and see a way to make it dovetail with a great deal for someone in France. And he sets up the deal. He risks no capital of his own, he produces nothing, owns no companies. He's a trader. He's always felt there was a certain spirit of adventure about the work. A careful flamboyance.

Today, pushing a button in the cherry-paneled elevator, Avrom walks into his office and says hello to Shahid, the young man who assists and is learning from him. Duval called. Shahid had to placate Fahoud. You want to set up a conference call with Syscom and the Stern brothers?

Avrom sketches out a strategy for the Syscom deal. Shahid leaves, and Avrom is about to sit down to work when, looking out the window at a patch of the Charles, he thinks, *Ben. Oh, Ben . . .* The grieving rushes through his chest, and in defense he whispers the first phrases of the mourners' Kaddish.

But praising God doesn't help. For he's not mourning Ben the way he did yesterday. His eyes are swollen with things he needs to say to him, ask him, hear from him, and there's no one there. He knows that Ben must be here in this office. He knows now that the world is drenched in past, he knows that simple versions of experience are laughable. The world isn't flat. It isn't even round. But Ben is gone. He sits, staring off into the ordinary air.

"Nothing new about Rwanda or Bosnia," Ben said on a walk one day. He could still walk. It was just after he understood what was happening to his body. "Look at Robert of Geneva, butcher for the pope. Late 1370s. He used Sir John Hawkwood to attack a little Italian city, Cesena or something, and they had the gall, the burghers, to resist. Robert swore an oath—clemency if they laid down their arms. So they did. Exactly like the Peasants Revolt in 1381 in England. Robert ordered the soldiers: kill everybody. Every fucking person. Sacred justice he called it. Some such shit. The soldiers even protested, but finally they closed the gates and slaughtered for two full days. They sold the children and killed the men and raped and killed the women. I mean thousands— seven, eight thousand dead. A small Holocaust. Fuck this life,

Ave. We hear about 'post-Holocaust theology,' as if the six million made everything different. It's no different. Generations of African slaves. Whole towns of Jews burned. The Armenians. The Cambodians. The Ukraine: Stalin starved millions—a country—to death. How do you pray past that? I don't get how to pray."

And Avrom remembers saying, "But that's why we pray."

"Look at me," Ben said. "I don't go around killing people. But I'm no saint, Ave. I'm full of hate sometimes. I'm a betrayer."

*I didn't get it. A "betrayer." What if Ben could have really said what he meant—maybe we could have invented something, some new form of love?—why not?*

He mourns, knowing how impossible that would have been. *What about Susan?*

And now, though nothing changes in the world he sees, a strange thing happens. Turning to his desk, he doesn't ponder his strategy for Syscom, doesn't make the list of calls he'd planned. He finds himself picking up the phone, punching in numbers, watching himself from outside. *Who am I calling?* At once, surprised, he knows—a client he hasn't dealt with in a year. And it proves just right, the call is timely. A deal starts to take shape, something out of nothing.

Looking up, he half feels, half sees, pools, pockets, billows of energy. They hover around his computer, around the files and telephone, and as he looks in any direction—say at a file drawer—he becomes aware of filaments of energy pulsing to telephone and computer.

Giddy, he rides the connections. Picking up the phone he knows who he has to call and punches in the number without having to look it up. So by the end of the morning he has a deal arranged for two containerloads of coffee from Nicaragua, a container shared by two electronics firms from Czechoslovakia, and another of machine tool parts to Hong Kong. In each case, he doesn't have to think. He sees the deal, he sees consequences and possibilities like a genius chess player on a board the size of the world. He rides the connections.

Yet by noon he's exhausted and in an odd way sad. Why sad? It's not Ben. He lies back in his leather reading chair and closes his eyes, and what he sees are the deals he's made, and they aren't numbers on a computer screen, they're busy with grief, there's sadness emanating from them, they speak to him of lives draining out of the bodies of men and women. Nothing's changed. It's a hundred years ago, it's seven hundred, deals are made and people earn their bread and pay their lives away.

He thinks, *Ben*. This is something he could talk to Ben about. He speaks to him now, a rush of awareness goes out to Ben. But Ben can't reply.

He has put together so many deals, taken upon himself responsibility for so much pain. Oh, life, too. Sure. He has provided livelihood. He knows that. It isn't guilt he feels but his own participation in the dance of pain and life.

The fingers of his heart fumble down inside himself. Eyes shut, he reads himself as braille. As if within him were a Torah. But he's not equipped to read it.

He reads: *Ben*. Ben. He remembers the afternoon, in New Haven, he first met Kristin. Ben got them together for lunch and then they visited the Museum of British Art—an exhibit of Pre-Raphaelite paintings—and Kristin played docent. There she was, waving her hand like a long-legged sprite, Ariel leading two big Calibans—Ben thick like a football player, he, Ave, long and gawky—through the rooms full of spiritualized beauties. Kristin's hair was chopped short that year. He couldn't take his eyes off her finely sculpted face; he found himself placing her face in the decorative canvases on the walls, she was so much more beautiful to him than the heavy-jawed beauties of Rossetti. But that wasn't it, it was her eyes. He saw truth in her eyes, simple truth, even when she was kidding Ben about his taste—oh, Ben played the boor, he charmed with a kind of parody crudeness—and maybe Ave's sense of her truth was intensified by her contrast to Ben. Truth, "soul," the kind of thing that Ben groaned at and Rossetti or Hunt faked. Even now he sees her eyes in the same way. And that's the funny thing—that professionally, she's an actress, that with him, too, she's been an actress, and yet he knows her, *knows* her—for a woman of truth.

And as that first afternoon went on and they had drinks somewhere and Ben patted them in blessing and went off, Ave gaped at her as if she were a most precious gift.

And that's what this is coming to. He recognizes that she was precisely that: a gift from Ben—he recognizes that even that first afternoon he knew. Something in the bluster of his friend, something in the pauses, the too-fast exchanges of banter, the way they didn't look at one another, was that it?—of *course* he knew they'd been lovers, of *course* he didn't let himself know he knew.

He looks up as Shahid, a recent graduate of Wharton, walks in with a stack of mail and a sheaf of faxes. Shahid's hands are full; he nudges the door shut with his hip, squeezes the mail under his arm while he sorts the faxes into piles, then puts the mail down on the desk. Avrom is amazed at what he wouldn't have noticed yesterday. All this *knowing* of the body's mind, not thought out— like a ballplayer running at the crack of the bat precisely to where the ball will arc. "Thanks, Shahid."

"Some morning, Avrom, some spectacular morning!"

Oh, he knew, knew they were lovers, though not that they became lovers again, but even *that*—there was always something charged between them. He knew. He was willing to take her on any terms offered. He knew; he didn't let himself know he knew.

He is swollen with knowledge. And with the knowledge

comes a fullness of anger—his generosity of spirit of last night gone—anger that washes through his chest and neck and face. He's touched a shorted electric wire—*that* potent, *that* unexpected. He could kill him over again. He sucks in breath to cope, and with the breath he enters an altered world. Feelings aren't "feelings"; they're palpable, visible, they surround him as thick lines of attachment, like threads of a monstrous spider, and he can't move. He senses them through his body, senses them blocking the room, barbed filaments joining him to Ben—*you betrayer, betrayer, what kind of friend?*—he pushes away the entanglements. If anyone came on him then—oh, he's aware of this—they'd see a crazy man pushing his hands through the air. He wants nothing to do with Ben, the son of a bitch, there in the corner. But oh my God he looks so full of grief. *Is that phony? My way to alleviate my pain?*

Maybe. But that's what he senses, Ben grieving in the corner, and he can't help joining him, mourning not for Ben this time but for the lost real impossible life between them, among the three of them. And as he begins to weep, sitting there at his rosewood desk, the strands grow soft and stop constraining him, the room is ordinary again except that Ben is there and the air between them has opened. It's like being inside a cubist canvas, except it's not flattened, it's like having your molecules suffused with light so that the boundaries are indistinct. What is this world?

He's sitting at his desk and at the same time on Ben's sailboat off Martha's Vineyard catching a look between Ben and Kristin, replaying that look during the morning to interpret it *any other way,* then hiding the look away.

Once: "How are you and Susan? You okay?"

"Okay, sure okay. You know. We fight. We like each other, Susan and me. We get along. We do okay in the sack if that's what you're asking."

"It wasn't."

"And . . . you and Kris?" Ben asked.

"Good."

"Good. That's good. Nice."

☾

Kristin is released—the tooth is pulled, she fits tongue into hollow. All morning there's been this giddy, anarchic feeling of having nothing to lose. Free fall. But then, taking a few minutes off from her work to straighten Micah's room, she feels in this hollow a pocket of grief. She straightens her study, already tidy, its books categorized, alphabetized; she rests in its neatness. Nothing to lose, no—but so much already lost. And when Avrom comes in unexpectedly after lunch, as she's preparing a theater exercise for her class, he suddenly becomes an embodiment of all that loss, the life she denied herself. Now there would be years ahead with the false surface of their life together stripped away—and what would be left? Only Micah. And she and Ave would turn into her parents, living separate lives in the same house.

He's standing at the door to her study. She glances his way and away again, not wanting to look at him because then she would have to feel his kindness. And it's his kindness that balks her, that's always balked her—because it made her believe in the value of their life together, it seduced her into pretense.

So when he says, "We need to talk," she snaps, furious, "It's too late for talk"—though this *is* the beginning of talk and she knows it. And, still lying, because after all it's Ave she's angry at, she tells him, "I'm furious at myself, Ave."

"For the deception?"

"Stop being my analyst! For not being with Ben. For not having the courage. I could have had all that life. Instead, I've lived a half-life."

"Have you? I don't think so. No." She spies him staring at her, or rather *through* her. He roams the little study, fingering her shelf of Samuel French acting editions. *"No,"* he says finally. "It's not true."

*"You* can't know. If I'd gone off with him . . . There were times we talked about it." And for just a moment the music of their being together plays in her. And quietly she adds, "He was the love of my life, Ave."

"You wouldn't believe how much life we've lived, you and I. You wouldn't believe it—how much life surrounds you now."

*"Please* don't give me that mystical crap, Ave!"

"I'm sorry. But it's not mystical. I see it, as tangibly as I see you."

"There was this passionate life between us, and I missed it."

"I wish we'd talked. Kris, love, Kris, maybe we could have invented something. We all did love one another. And the thing is—Kris, I knew."

"You *didn't* know. Oh, bullshit you knew."

"I saw looks, there were moments you were on the phone and suddenly blanched when I walked in. I turned the other way. I knew. I turned the other way. I'm ashamed. I made you take the whole burden."

She refuses to give him even this. "But *talk*—what would have been the good?" she says. "Charlie and Steve, Susan too, and you and me. There was too much at stake. You see, the thing is," Kris says, and now she's coping with tears, "we did the right fucking thing." She says "fucking," she recognizes, in Ben's voice.

"And there's Micah," Ave adds.

*"And* Micah. Micah. Micah's why we stopped. Ave? I can't swear who's his father."

Now she waits, getting sick to her stomach through a long silence, before he says, "I am. I'm his father."

"We hardly saw each other by then. You *are.* Oh, but Ave, Ave, I want to go backward and live the other life. I don't know how we can stay married now." She says this to him because he is, after all, the closest adult in the world to her; furious at Avrom her husband, she says it to Avrom her friend.

"Because we *are* married. We were all so enmeshed. We should have talked."

"I don't know."

"The trouble with the dead, you can talk to them but they can't answer. I want to invent a different spiritual universe."

"Stop! Grow up."

"Ben told me the same. One day I said to Ben, 'Maybe there's something to the reports about the light you move toward as you die.' And he still had the strength to get pissed. 'We can talk about God, okay, but don't give me any of that white light crap! Don't hoke it up, Ave.'"

At this she had to laugh. And she felt the impulse to hold him and soothe Avrom and be soothed, but, afraid it would be seen as begging absolution, she held back.

Now he sits on the edge of her desk and holds out his hands, open, as if he's waiting beneath a tree to break a child's fall from a high place. She closes her file and shuts down the computer and his hands are still there, fingers stretched out to her. With a sigh of irritation she gives him her hands as if they were foreign objects.

He has this diffuse gaze *into* her—*smarmy,* she thinks—that makes her yank her hands away again. *I won't let you use me this way.*

He says, "For a while this morning it was gone, but now it's always there. I wish I could bring you into it with me."

"I'll stay where I am, thanks."

"Though there's nowhere to bring you. It's just the ordinary world," he says. "You're already there." He stands up and, in a kind of giddy, spurious victory, tilting up his face, he holds his hands out, fingers spread, first as if he were riding the air, then as if he were connected by each finger to—she doesn't know what.

"You're spooking me," Kristin says very quietly. "Please."

"It's not like that. Kris. Come inside. We're so absolutely connected here. It's beautiful if you let it be."

"What are you doing with your eyes like that? Please. Ave? Be careful you don't go too far with this. Please. Oh, Ave." She reaches out to pull his hands to her. "It's been a terrible time, for you. I know. Such a terrible time. Oh, honey . . . you'll be all right." But what *makes* it all right, suddenly all right, is that his craziness, this crazy way of handling pain, has touched her. For a moment the word, *honey,* releases its sweetness in her. This sweetness, the tenderness she feels, her longing to soothe, makes her think, why, there must be something between them to make her care like this. This dear fool. This complicated, crazy man.

"Are you seeing Ben now?" she asks.

"Here, and here, and here," he gestures, a magician pulling small change out of the air. "But it's more than that, Kris. I'm in touch. It's like being in this other country."

"All right," she says, and she reaches up to touch the fingers of his other hand.

☾

There's no way to take her here, and yet *here* is where she is, Kristin; he isn't even separate from her; they interpenetrate. She breathes him in, he breathes her in. Then how can she not be here with him? He breathes Ben in, he breathes Ben out. The air is also thick with grief that finds its way into Avrom's open skin. Nerve gas, used to murder whole villages of Kurds. Smoke that rose up the chimneys at Buchenwald, still in this air. It must be here.

Ben wanted to feel like a tough guy; he chose to stare down murder. And so I didn't have to, he did it for me. He did the dying, too. I wish he could have said, *Kristin and me,* and I could have said, *I know, I know.* It seems so much less difficult a thing than murder.

*I need to speak to him about that.*

The study is suffused with Ben and with the loss of Ben. And Kristin—Ave sees Kristin as if meeting her for the first time. He's never known her, known that she's this much music. She's a new love. She's almost a different species; it takes his breath away. And yet he can read the codes of pulse in her wrist. She's a grad student sitting cross-legged on a blanket in the grass, examining his face shrewdly just as they're about to make love the first time, she's the nine-month woman whose belly shone with oil from his fingers, belly that shifted with Micah's hip or elbow, and he pressed his ear there to hear the strange heart singing. She's a young woman who knows she can be a great actress and at the same time the teacher who still performs but has never established an acting career. And she's the old woman he will be living with in twenty years—he sees that possibility in the room, too. And Ben is with them and so is the loss of Ben.

Strands of grief and love connect them all to one another. He doesn't say to her: *The boundaries are so blurred. Between me and Ben. Between dead and living. Be with me. I'm all you'll have of him.* But Avrom mourns for Ben, mourns in a different way now, the way one mourns for one's own lost possibilities.

The air is open and full of dreams, the walls and books pulse with their talk, and the stained-glass lamp over the desk and the secondhand desk itself and the brass candlestick of her mother's and the worn Turkish carpet, they break open and spill their constitutive dreams, dreams that permeate the almost-visible air. He feels now, right now, he is making something, completing something, doing real work by his openness to the permeable air, *making* the world of wholeness he and Ben mourned for. Is it wishful seeing? The dark greens and reds of the carpet say themselves in waves to his eyes. If I'm crazy it doesn't matter much.

Not to frighten Kristin, he says it only in his heart to Ben, *Talk to me.* And Ben does "talk"—Avrom isn't hearing voices, he's feeling the words from Ben's many presences: friend teaching him to sail, friend who puzzles out a passage from Torah with him, deceiver who tried to tell him. But what Ben can't say is anything new. *Only I can do that, now,* Ave thinks. And so he says it, aloud: "I survived, not you. I have to tell you, I'm glad of it."

"Is that it?" Kristin says. "Is it so terrible to survive?"

He doesn't answer. He says, "Please?" and helps her up from the desk to lead her to her daybed. She says, "How can we do it? How can we stay married?" but she doesn't resist him. He knows very well she thinks she's humoring him, placating, but he knows, too, that in this *other* place in which even the air has depth and the depth gushes out through its secret pores, they are very close, so close that he's a little afraid. He isn't sure he knows where he leaves off and she begins, though she's also an alien creature. They sit cross-legged on the bed together the way they do sometimes before sleep, and he says, "The bed is very crowded."

"*Not* crowded. It's just us. Just us. Please, Ave."

"Well, I suppose beds always are, that's the way it is with beds." Tentatively, he strokes the nape of her neck. Tenderness coats his fingers. And with the touch, his fear subsides.

# *Muscles*

*His* father—bull of a man, red-faced and thick of neck, wearing sloppy old pants and worn-out business shirt, the collar frayed—carried the pail of soapy hot water, Ben the sponges and a pail of clear warm water. "C'mon, c'mon, c'mon."

Ben's mother warned as the elevator doors closed, "Leo—try to be decent with your son! Oh—and be sure to remember me to your charming brother." Down the elevator and up the street to wherever the car was parked.

This was the 1950s, New York City, West Eighty-fourth off Columbus, where they'd moved from Jackson Heights.

When he was eight, and still when he was fifteen, Ben promised himself he'd stay home on Sunday and play sick or say he had homework. Why was it he always went along? To show his father he was loyal to the activities of men? Did he really believe that this time he'd scrub the old Chevy without missing bug spots, wouldn't waste the soapy water or the clean? wouldn't hear his father holler in that operatic baritone—you could hear it a hundred yards off—"If you're gonna slop up the car like that, forget the whole goddamn thing. You just leave soap film"?

Some Sundays Ben blew up and stormed off, not looking at his father, cursing to himself. More often, he ended up arms folded, leaning as if bored against a car. Yet secretly he watched his two-hundred-pound father, pail in one hand, sponge in the other, scrub that car with every bit of his amazing force, grunting his breath, cursing the son-of-a-bitch Chevy as if it were trying to defeat him by staying dirty.

Now, fifty years later, he thinks of the man in Homeric terms, like a drawing of Achilles by Leonard Baskin, all that crude, passionate force expended so purely but so pitifully on such an inadequate object. To be in the presence of that angry power!

Say it's 1955, late spring, Ben is fifteen, and after a humiliating half hour with sponges and pails, he was Silent Cal, driving alongside his father to a pickup softball game in Central Park, and his father, softened now that the car is clean, was trying to appease him with sweet talk. "Ahh, you know me, Ben. I'm a fussy son of a bitch. I know it. We both know it. You don't mind your old broken-down father, do you?"

And Ben said, as he was meant to say, "It's okay, you just get excited. You've got your ways you want things done."

"That's just it exactly. You know I'm nuts about you."

They parked on Central Park West. It was the first Sunday they were trying this pickup game, so Leo Kagan was nervous, clearing his throat a lot and spitting it out on the grass, pounding fist into glove, saying, "Hey, straighten up, Ben. Look like a ballplayer. You want to get picked, don't you?"

This was the year Ben grew almost an inch a month. He used to be pudgy; now he was skinny. But fat or skinny, he couldn't play softball, not well enough to be here. He stood in the clump of men and older teenagers getting looked over by the captains.

Leo Kagan was in his early sixties, gray-haired and heavy-gutted, and nobody here knew him. He banged his fist into Ben's side at each pick as if saying, *Good pick, good pick*—or else, *What? That schmuck? Looks like a pansy.* Ben knew which by the rhythm of the poke.

Ben got chosen with only a few players left standing, his father on the very last round. Only a few young kids left at the end.

"Hey, Pops, you want right field? Or can you maybe pitch?" Slow-pitch softball—they figured maybe he'd be a steady slow-ball pitching machine, but Leo said, "How about first base? That's my position."

And because he was an old guy and they didn't want to insult him, somebody shrugged, "Let's try you out. A little pepper." And they tossed the ball around and made Leo reach, and he pulled them in from goddamn all over, even jumping, even down in the dirt. "Okay, Pops, you've got first."

Ben was on the other team and didn't get up in the first inning. In right field he stood rocking. Second inning he popped up; his father said, "Good piece of the ball, Ben. Next time!"

His father got up bottom of the second, middle of a rally, two on, one out, and slammed the first pitch way over the head of the left fielder. Way the hell out, over any fence they could have put in that field, but there was no fence, and the left fielder took off after the ball, and Leo, slow as he was, trudging heavy around the bases, puffed home.

And so it went. Ben got a single in the eighth, a fluke off the tip of the bat. And his father played perfect first base, hit three home runs, though the fielders played him farther and farther back, and the center fielder barely got his glove on another. They slapped his father on the back, asked him to come back, and he was grinning.

Only when they were heading back to the car did Ben start to feel his own failure. At first his father was in too good a mood to care. "You see me smack that son of a bitch? They didn't know who the hell they were dealing with. You see me smack that third one? Your old dad ain't got no legs. But can I belt that son of a bitch?"

"That was something. I guess next time they won't wait to pick you."

"They can kiss my ass, Ben. Next time, it's me picking them."

"Great! Well, you're a ringer, you were semi-pro."

"That's right. . . . So how is it *you* can't hit worth a damn? The thing is, you got to watch me, the way I keep my eye on the ball all the way in, the way I get my shoulders into it. Vooomh! Maybe we'll go out this week and practice. If I can get off a little early? What do you think? You game?"

"You're the ballplayer in the family, Dad."

"Well, we're different, right? But don't think I'm not proud of you, Ben. When they handed out the brains, you and my brother got all they had to go around."

Leo Kagan was in high spirits all through the park, but when he saw his clean black car, it was as if his real life came back to him; his eyes dulled, his face seemed to lose definition.

"You think we ought to go home and change?" Ben asked, trying to bring him back.

"Nah. Cy says, your uncle says, 'Come as you are.' He says, 'Don't stand on no ceremony with me.' Anyway, there's no time. The big guy's leaving to play golf at one o'clock. I brought us a couple of clean shirts and pants and a comb. We can change in the car." He took out a handkerchief and mopped his own face, then used the sweat to wash the dirt off Ben's.

"I thought you were supposed to be getting a haircut," Leo Kagan said as he jammed the car through its changes. "Look at your hair! I can't trust your mother to keep her word. . . . God-damn traffic for a Sunday! And they don't know how to drive. This city is getting to be unlivable. We'll cut across at Fifty-sixth."

Uncle Cy, recently divorced, was staying temporarily at the War-wick; his wife had "kicked him out on his ear," Ben's mother said, "because he *wasn't a real man with her,* you understand me, Ben?"

Ben didn't understand. Who could be more powerful than Uncle Cy? Ben saw his father as a clumsy giant of some strange race. But his uncle!—Uncle Cy, though no athlete, was taller than his older brother Leo, more handsome, with a Dick Tracy chin he carried high and beautiful silver hair usually covered by a Stetson. He strode through the sonofabitch city like the cattle baron in westerns, though he grew up in Chicago, an immigrant kid, and the only West he'd seen was once on the train to Los Angeles. A poor Jewish kid from Chicago who happened to be smart, he learned to be a courtroom stenographer at fourteen, became an officer during the First World War directly out of civilian life, landing a job in Washington as secretary to a general.

This general must have given him a smattering of style—after all, what could a kid like that, his father a cigar roller, his mother a boardinghouse keeper, know about clothes, about food, about business talks and deals? Yet by 1926 Cy was working for himself, building a tire sales operation, starting on not much more than a phony slogan—"World's Largest Distributor"—and by the time Ben was born, Cy was a millionaire owning half a city block in the West Forties. No longer a Jew—his name Colburn now—he had made himself into the American "sport" of his youth, dapper but street-smart. He blended his own whiskey from unblended imports, spent a part of the racing season at Saratoga. But none of that expressed the power he gave off, power that made Ben—in spite of himself, in spite of the loyalty he felt to his mother *("That uncle of yours has ruined my life")*—feel more alive just to be in his uncle's presence.

"Mr. Colburn is expecting you." In the gilt-framed mirrors at the Warwick he saw himself reflected as if he were another boy. His father had spit on the comb and wet down his hair, a severe part too near the middle. Now Leo stopped and looked Ben over. Ben stepped outside his body to see himself with his father's eyes. But in turn, his father was seeing Ben not with his own eyes but with the eyes of his brother, Ben's uncle. So he and his father both disappeared, and the only eyes between them belonged to the uncle/brother they imagined.

While they waited for the elevator, Leo Kagan kept talking. "If the big guy asks, you tell him how good you're doing in school. Tell him math, tell him history. He don't believe in literature if you get me. Frankly, Ben, he's grooming you."

In the elevator Leo squirmed inside his clothes, stuck two fingers into his collar. *My poor father, my poor, big father.* Ben watched the little light rising through the glass numbers.

"Come on in, this here's the president's office and I'm the god-damn president, so what're you waiting for?"

Cy sat at the window, leg crossed at the knee, in a crisp blue cotton-knit shirt, pale beige linen pants, brown and white golf shoes. The King of Fifth Avenue. Ben knew he'd just set himself into that pose to seem relaxed and in charge—but even knowing, still he was charmed.

It was the room of a transient. There were file boxes and suit-cases piled up in the corners. On two open card tables were stacks of papers. The furniture was just expensive, pompous hotel fur-niture. Still, this was the real world. Ben bathed in it.

"Don't an uncle get a handshake, Ben?"

And Ben, about to plant a nephew's kiss on his uncle's fresh-shaved cheek, stuck out a hand. *Don't an uncle get . . .* It was Chi-cago street talk, held on to the way a Frenchman may hold on to a charming accent. The bad grammar was his uncle coming on tough and American, buddy to gangsters, no Jew. And his father copied it. Once, Ben tested his uncle. He said about a second-rate pitcher, "He ain't nothin'." And Cy said, "Christ, haven't they taught you better English than *that?*"

The funny thing was, Uncle Cy wanted *him* to be cultivated. He wanted Ben to attend an Ivy League school and turn into the kind of person both brothers made fun of. His father truly wanted a jock for a son. Cy wanted a nephew who was going to "become something."

"We've just been playing softball, the kid and me," his father said. "Tell your uncle."

"Dad was fantastic. He hit three home runs."

"Wellll, I'll tell you," his uncle sighed, a philosophical sigh, a profound sigh. "After you grow up, who gives a good goddamn if you can hit a home run? See what I'm saying?"

"That's what I tell the kid," Leo said. "He feels bad he can't play like his old dad, but look where the hell that got me." Ben saw his father waiting for a grin. It didn't come. His father picked at the dirt under his nails.

Deadpan, Uncle Cy stood up and picked at the things on his desk. Taking up a file, he began filing his nails. Imagine, underneath the rest of this conversation, the rasp of a file. "What's the matter, Leo? You saying you don't appreciate your job?"

"Sure, I appreciate my job, I like my job, I do a good job for you, Cy."

"Because if that wife of yours is dissatisfied, you just tell me and we can call it quits anytime, no hard feelings."

"She's got nothing to do with it. She doesn't say a goddamn thing. I wouldn't let her."

"You know," Cy said, "you're my brother, and I'd love to come over to the house more. . . . "

"Cy, the boy here—"

"What's he—some little kid that he can't hear what's going on? You and I were out in the real world we were his age. We were supporting Mom and Dad."

"Exactly. That was another generation entirely."

"I'm not saying he shouldn't get an education. Who the hell's sending him through private school?"

"You are, Cy."

"I'm saying, let him know that his wonderful mother—who he should be loyal to, I'm not saying he shouldn't—can sometimes be one royal pain in the anatomy with her fantasies about what I owe you."

"You don't owe me a thing."

"Hey. Do you think I owe you, Leo?"

"You do okay by me. You're my brother."

"You bet I'm your brother. You think otherwise I'd put up with you?—Only kidding, Ben. Your pop is some salesman, he's some manager, no kidding. But listen—you guys got here too late for lunch. I got to play golf with some hoity-toity sonofabitches. I hate to hurry you out of here. Leo, do me a favor, can you drive out to Great Neck and pick up a signed contract for me from old man Lipman?"

"Sure, but it's Sunday, Cy. I figured me and the boy—"

Cy didn't say anything. He put away his nail file, picked up his attaché case, and got his golf clubs out of the closet. He checked his watch.

"Well," Ben's father said, "how about a little later on, maybe four, four-thirty? Ben and me can go out to LaGuardia on the way, watch the planes come in. Or—I c'd go over earlier—"

"You just bring me the contract early tonight so I can get started on it, okay, Leo? You remember how to get to Lipman's?"

"Sure I do."

"Your father, Ben, is one loyal brother. I dragged him to New York from Chicago when I started this operation. If I hadn't, you know where you'd'a grown up? In some triple-decker in Chicago, the son of a shoe salesman. Hell, nothing wrong with that. But I knew I needed somebody I could trust. You get me?" And beaming, he put his arm around his older brother's shoulder. To Ben it looked as if his father—grinning, melting under Cy's touch—constricted physically. Shrank.

Then they were out the door, his father behind him, one hand on Ben's shoulder, patting.

"He knows he can rely on me for little things, Ben. So he can rely on me for the big ones. You get me?"

Cold as stone, Ben watched the gold arrow above the elevator fall.

"Ben? What's the matter? You mad because I said you just played 'okay'?"

Ben shook his head. All the way down in the elevator he didn't look at his father. In the lobby his father grabbed onto him. "Hey, in fact, in fact you're getting to be one sweet little ballplayer. Your fielding's a hundred times better than last year."

"So? You think I care? Somebody hits a round object with a wooden stick? You think I care?"

"What kind of crap are you talking?"

"Why does my uncle hate you so much? Why do you let him get away with that shit?"

"You watch your mouth. You been listening to your mother?"

Ben guffawed. He took off through the lobby. Leo followed. Ben thought about losing his father—split for Columbus Circle and take the subway home. But why *now*, why was he so angry *now*? After all—the poor bastard! Ben felt lousy, heartless. Fishing down into himself he felt a nibble—something—what? Slowing, he let his father catch up.

"You gone crazy? Tell me. You gone nuts or something? My brother barks a little, I know how he can get on his high horse—what, do you take him so seriously?"

"That phony!" Ben yelled at the corner of Sixth and Fifty-fifth.

"Shh!" Leo took Ben by the elbow and spoke confidentially. "Sure. Phony is right. I'm glad you spotted that. You take for instance his pansy clothes. Yellow pants? Imagine wearing prissy clothes like that. That guy makes believe he's tough. Back in Chicago I had to protect him. He couldn't walk to school without his big brother. He was something of a candy-ass, your uncle. But the kids stayed clear. They knew—I hit 'em, they stay down. Right? Am I right?" He laughed and chucked Ben under the jaw.

"Well," Ben said, "*it's not that way now.*"

"What the hell do you know about it?"

"Muscles. You've got big muscles. So what? You still got a lousy old car and you scrub and scrub till the paint's half off and your phony brother tells you what to do on a Sunday."

His father didn't get red in the face and yell. He just picked at his teeth with a fingernail. It took him a while to find his keys, and a while for him to open the door. Leaning, he opened the passenger side.

They were silent all the way out to LaGuardia. Ben wished he could unsay it; still, he had a right! It was true! He felt the tingling of victory in the long war with his father. It wasn't until Leo Kagan put a dime in the turnstile to the spectators' deck and, as always, slipped Ben in for free on the same turn, not until they stood watching the big DC-8s and Constellations taking off in the vibrating air that Ben saw what was *new,* saw why beneath everything, he felt so terrible:

Uncle Cy had done it as a piece of *theater*—for Ben. Ben was the intended audience for his uncle's power and his father's shame. That was new.

His uncle was saying, *Look how leaky that vessel is.* Well, it was tempting—to see his uncle fighting on his side against his cloddish tub of a father. Abandon ship.

But as the shining planes rose through their powerful guttural growl and whine, he felt himself sink, as if he, too, were leaky and his substance were seeping away through the cracks. Victorious, he felt diminished.

His father, leaning his bulk on the rail, was watching men in mechanics' zip-up suits load luggage from a cart to the belly of a Constellation. Ben leaned down to watch with him, and his father, sensing he could say something, knowing that sooner or later he *had* to say something, pointed, "Look at that—they do one hell of a job, those guys."

"Like the tire changers down at work."

"Sure."

A plane touched down; they watched it glide away from

them. "I want to say, I'm sorry, Dad. What I said before. It's no big deal you let him get away with stuff. It's just because . . . you're *loyal* to him. He's your brother," Ben said, dusting off the words his father used when Ben's mother snapped at him for "*letting that brother of yours walk all over you.*"

But today, looking not at Ben but at the planes, he said, "No, you're right. When you're right you're right. I let him get away with murder. He's no goddamn good, my brother. I wasn't so scared, I'd've walked out on him. But I got a family."

"What about this Jimmy MacMillan you could go work with?"

"Your mother's dreaming. Look, Ben, your mother's a goddamn wonderful woman. She's worth ten of my brother. Don't you think I know that? But Jimmy MacMillan, that was years ago. 1946. I'm no kid, Ben. Who wants a new man sixty-three years old? You get me?"

"Sure."

"You're a smart boy. You don't ever let him get his hands on you."

"Don't worry. . . . I'm sorry what I said. About muscles."

"S'okay. We'll play softball next Sunday, okay? I'll get you on my team. Hey—but you look at this old car," he said, patting the '46 Chevy. "What's wrong for an old car?"

"Sure. You really keep it up."

"On the way to old man Lipman's, you want, we can stop for a soda."

But on the way to Lipman's house, Leo forgot the soda; he brooded. Getting back to the city, in heavy traffic on the Triborough, Leo hunched in a rage against the stupid drivers. By the time he got off at Ninety-sixth and headed west, he was honking and cursing. And when the guy in the big Chrysler in front of him dawdled and cost them both the light, Leo held his hand down on the horn and his face got red.

Then the other driver did a dumb thing—he gave Leo an upraised middle finger. You didn't do that to Leo Kagan. He stepped out of his car, put his big body against the Chrysler, and rocked the car, and when the driver, in gray suit and fedora, pushed down the lock, Leo pounded on the side window and the windshield, yelling, "You come outta there—I'm gonna beat the living crap outta you!" Not an invitation any sane New Yorker was likely to accept. Ben had seen the same thing five, ten times, and never had anyone come out—nor even looked his father's way.

At the green light the Chrysler took off, throwing Leo back a little. Cars behind started honking. Leo got in and chased the Chrysler up the block, but when it turned south on Park, he gave up the chase with a laugh. "I scared the jerk off." He sat back, cleared his throat, growled. "It's lucky for that guy he didn't start something."

Ben didn't say anything. His father stopped for cold cuts on the way home. A block from the house, miraculously Leo found a space good for Monday, and he pulled in. Ben saw his new fielder's mitt on the back seat. Quick, he shoved it under the front seat; to disguise what he was doing, he collected the pails and brushes and sponges. His father, baseball clothes over his arm, wanted to get back to the *Journal American,* to Sunday cold cuts, to Walter Winchell and Jack Benny. Ben trudged after him up the street, staring at the shiny cloth on the seat of his pants.

*Son of a shoe salesman,* he thought. He'd always known his father had sold shoes, but something about the way his uncle put it made him think about shoes. How his father cared so much that Ben's shoes were tied just so. And until he was a big kid, maybe seven or eight, much too old, his father would grump, "Let me tie your shoes *right*," and Ben would have to sit on the edge of the bed and his father would bend a little and, sweating with the effort, take the boy's right shoe into his own crotch and tie it firmly; and then the left, tie it firmly. It was an expression of tenderness and professional competence.

He wished his father had stayed in Chicago. What was so wrong with being a shoe salesman?

It was his father who traditionally bought and laid out the cold cuts on a Sunday evening. "Look at that roast beef," he'd sing out as he slapped the meat onto the blue willow platter and spread out the slices to look more impressive. "Is that some roast beef? Fit for a king. At least one time a week I get the kind of rye bread I can eat."

Not tonight. Tonight, he was quiet. He left the waxed paper under the meats and made no claims.

At dinner, Ben's mother, chain-smoking, looking ravaged for a Sunday spent with the papers, asked him, "Well? How did it go with your big-shot brother? Did he serve you a nice lunch? I suppose he asked graciously about me?"

"Never mind about my brother. He's my problem."

"Oh, no, my dear. He's very much *my* problem, don't you think? That man—why, he isn't fit to kiss my foot." And then her uplifted chin—a breakwater against the indignities of living a mediocre life, of being forced to keep track of every dollar—fell to her chest. She looked as if she were praying; Ben knew she was wrapping herself in her griefs.

"Listen, you—" Leo growled. "He knows what you are, my brother. All you're interested in are the material things you can't have."

Even at fifteen, Ben knew these were not Leo's own words. Fifty years later, Ben knows, too, how *inaccurate* those words were. What his mother hungered for wasn't really material at all.

Fed up, this night in 1955, with her life, she ground out her cigarette in the food he'd provided and she couldn't eat. She sat nodding, nodding, nodding, like a crazy person. "Say, I'll tell you what," she said hoarsely. "Why don't you and your brother cut me up and eat me? No, really. 'Rahlly,' as Bette Davis says. Then he can cut your salary."

Ben knew the next line—*You're so goddamn jealous.* Something like that. But his father didn't yell that. Instead, he cleared his throat, as if a truck engine were revving up, cleared his throat and stood, heavily, brushing the crumbs off his shirt front, as if he were about to make an after-dinner speech. A big man filling the kitchen.

They sat there and looked at him. Now, a little as if he were on stage, Leo walked into the living room and picked up the phone. Usually, from anywhere in the house you could hear everything Leo Kagan said on the phone. Not tonight. Tonight the words were quiet. Then Leo came back and said nothing and sat down.

"Well, my dear," Ben's mother said, "well, my dear, and did you tell your brother how terrible I am?"

"You?" he said quietly. "It had nothing to do with you. I told him I couldn't get out tonight. I said to him, 'Cy, I got you your contract. You want to look it over, you're gonna have to stop by.'"

"You *said* that?" Ben asked.

And now, fifty years later, Ben holds his breath remembering, though at the time he didn't know that he knew how extraordinary it was, that moment of quiet in the kitchen.

"Sure, that's what I told him. Cy said, 'Okay, bring it to work in the morning.' He wasn't too happy."

"Dad. You told him *that?*"

Leo snapped—"Yeah. What's the big deal, Ben? I'm *tired.* I played hard today. Did you tell your mother about the game I played? Anyway, this is none of your business."

With the Yiddish intonations that indicated she was offering communal truth, truth of all mothers, she asked, "So why can't you be decent to your only son?"

That did it. The quiet in the kitchen was over. "I don't want another goddamn word out of you," Leo yelled at her. He shoved away his plate. He cracked his finger joints and stood, big-boned man ready for the usual fight.

Ben shoved meat between two slices of rye and took the plate back to his room. A magazine reproduction of *Starry Night* had come loose from the wall at one corner; he pressed the tape. The walls needed painting. Maybe he could cover them with movie posters? He put on his radio, the classical station he'd begun to listen to, and played it loud enough to blur the voices, not quite loud enough to make his father bang on the door and crack the paint some more.

She'd left his laundry, folded, on the bed. She'd sewn his pants with fine stitches that couldn't have mattered less to him. But he ran his fingers over her work. Voices! He turned up the music.

The voices, they seeped in. He lay on his bed and took up a history book, but the words wouldn't stay together. The room was carrying him through space—dizzying!—this rickety boat he'd nailed and glued. It was all he had; it could carry him only so far. He chewed his sandwich of meat and grief; with the clenching of the muscles of his jaw, his will coalesced and knotted. Outside, waves of anguish—door slammings, shouts, guttural threats—smashed at the leaky walls.

# Time Exposure

*N*ow, half a century later, he's been thinking what it must have cost her, her transformation from little Jewish girl in Kishnief in the early years of the century to a modern American woman—a career woman in New York—and then to fade, like a shooting star burning out, into marriage with "your poor fool of a father."

The staircase to his study is lined on both walls with family photographs. One side of the family on each side of the stairs— his father's side, his mother's. Facing each other now: His father in shirtsleeves, an idealistic-looking boy, and his younger brother with tough, cynical grin, against a brick wall in Chicago, and with them their father in short hair and moustache, dapper little man, his hands on the shoulders of his sons. And across the stairway, Ben's mother, black hair in ringlets, older brothers and sisters surrounding her, she the youngest, the pet. Her father, in skull-cap, with heavy beard and intense, wise eyes. Her mother looks thick like a peasant; hard work shows on her face even in this studio portrait. His father's family looks American; his mother's,

like immigrant Jews. Black coats, heavy silk dresses. For his
mother to turn herself into a bright, gay woman of the late twenties, a successful fashion buyer, must have been like skipping a
century. To love and marry and relapse into her mother's role
must have felt a relief, as well as a failure.

Now he understands; it's like replaying a dialogue secretly
taped and then replayed, and this time you *get* it: the way she'd
hear swing music on the old Victrola radio, mahogany case like a
miniature gothic church, and dance in circles on the kitchen li-
noleum, flirting with an elegant, invisible partner, singing in her
throaty cigarette voice and smiling a public smile. "You think
your mother is old-fashioned, don't you? You don't think I'm a
modern woman?"

Her only audience, Ben waited—amused, critical, understanding the pretenses but not the need for those pretenses.

"God grant me long life as true as I'm standing here I was in
Flo Ziegfeld's apartment—some apartment, let me tell you—
over the theater, and he said to me, 'Myra, you're something special. You know what's going on. Where did your family come
from?'

"'From Russia, Mr. Ziegfeld,' I told him. 'I was born in Kishnief.' Well, the whole world knew Kishnief because of the terrible
pogrom. Before I was born.

"'No!' he said. I said, 'Yes, Mr. Ziegfeld. From Russia. I came
to America when I was five.' 'My God,' he said, 'and you are every
bit an American girl.'"

This was like getting a Ph.D. in American Girliana. Did Ziegfeld really say that? It doesn't matter; it's her imagination of herself that matters.

"'Myra,' Flo Ziegfeld said to me, 'if you ever want to come to
work for me'—he meant in the Follies—'you just come to see
me.' Of course, he was joking—would your mother ever do such
a thing? But I charmed him. *Well?* You don't think so?"

She waited for her son to dare laugh at her.

"What? You don't think your mother used to be beautiful?

You think I was always a *hausfrau* and a frump?" She'd find a couple of quarters in the pocket of her housedress (tips for the deliv-
ery boys) and place one between her knees, one between her
calves. "You see? This is how Ziegfeld made his girls stand. To test
their legs, *ferstaste?*"

Once, she sighed, once she sailed first-class on the *France* to
France and ate at the captain's table. A Rothschild fell in love with
her. And now look—look how she'd come down in the world.
"Your poor father. A slave to his brother. But a better man God
never made. He can't help being what he is. I can't help being what
I am. I fell in love. Do me something—your mother fell in love."

And so now, because of love, they lived in Jackson Heights,
Long Island—in a dismal, red-brick apartment building on a
street of red-brick apartment buildings. The wrong side of the
East River, Manhattan a short but shameful ride away.

"He means well, the poor fool. Can he help being what he is?"

"And now!" she'd sing out. "*Voila!* Isn't your mother a stunning
woman?" Hands lifted: a statue. Her one good black linen outfit,
a blue silk scarf at her throat.

"It's true, Ben," his father would roar. "She's a goddamn
stunning woman and look what a bum she married."

He called in reservations at the Sea Fare in the name of
"Judge Kagan." They drove the 1940 Pontiac, obsessively polished, into Manhattan over the Queensboro Bridge. From the
bridge, the downtown lights flashed like jewels his mother
wasn't wearing.

He was an actor, not a patron, at the Sea Fare: Leo Kagan as
"Judge" Kagan. Ben was fearful lest the headwaiter unmask
him—"You, a judge? Don't you know it's against the law to im-
personate a judge?" But no, it was always, "Follow me. Please,
Judge." The judge winked his way.

Five times at least during the meal his father computed, re-
computed, the waiter's tip. "We're getting pretty decent service,
right, Ben?" Or else, he'd flash the fancy racetrack watch his uncle

Cy gave him for his birthday. "You see how slow he is with the bread and butter? I can predict what kind of tip that schmuck is going to wind up with."

And, cupping his hand so his mother could pretend not to hear, he'd whisper, "I wouldn't give that schmuck the sweat off my balls."

Partly, it was spending the money; partly, it was having to be on his best behavior in front of his wife. But always, on the way home, things fell apart. Some driver would pass him or squeeze him over. Leo Kagan would pull alongside and yell out the window, "Who gave you a goddamned license? You faggot! You ought to have your head examined."

Now his wife would refuse to recognize his existence, and that would drive him wild. He'd thump the dash, explain and explain, "That sonofabitch—did you see him cut me off?"

She'd sigh, in her cultured, near-British voice, "Well, and *isn't* it nice weather, Ben? D'you think it's likely to rain tomorrow?"

Louder, louder, he'd explain. Finally, "Goddamned woman! Goddamn you!" It was a war. Only now Ben understands: In this roundabout way he played out the drama of his own worthlessness. He needed to goad her into despising him—so that then he could hate her for despising him and not have to hate himself so much? Wasn't that it? And she used *him* to excuse her retreat from complicated modern America. So that both of them could be justified in how they imagined their lives.

Next morning, she'd be her most charming, regal self, telling stories.

"You think I'm your ordinary housewife?" she'd say over breakfast. "Listen: when you were born, old man Bonwit, God rest his soul, called me up to see him. I'd been away from the business for three, four years. Well. I dressed in my smartest suit— you'll laugh, darling, there was a moth hole in the collar, I wore a brooch to hide it—and I took a cab down to Bonwit's. When I came in, his secretary announced me, and I could hear his voice over the intercom, 'Myra Bresloff? Send her in, send her in.' Well. So I went in, he stood up from his desk and took both my hands. 'Myra Bresloff. Myra Bresloff.' I can see him to this day. A little man growing bald—but *smart*. 'I'm Myra Kagan now, Mr. Bonwit,' I told him. 'Myra, you can name your price.' 'How sweet you are,' I told old man Bonwit, 'but I have a little boy, my dear, and I believe a woman belongs with her family.' 'Is there nothing I can do to change your mind?' 'If anyone could, you could,' I told him. 'But my *family*.' 'And I admire that, Myra. Every woman should take lessons from you.' So—that was that, you understand. *You* came first. But when I got home that afternoon, there was a bouquet of flowers waiting. *That* was a big man. Well—so you came first. You see? Now, what kind of mother do you have?"

"A bitter mother."

"Nonsense. Bitter? I'm a happy wife and mother."

When she was just twenty-three, twenty-four, old man Bonwit sent her to Paris for the first time; then he sent her every spring to preview the fall lines. She stayed at the Georges Cinq. Rich men danced with her; coming back to the hotel, she would find a dozen roses and no card and not know which of a half-dozen men to thank. But she married "your poor father" and expected he'd be rich someday. Only it turned out—"funny how things turn out"—he was just a slave to his younger brother. "An unsung hero," she'd praise him when she wasn't feeling bitter. "That *grubyom*, that peasant!" she'd snap when she was. "My poor father wouldn't sleep in his grave. Did you know he brought me up like a son? To read Hebrew, to say the prayers. He had a great, long beard—well, in those days, you understand. He held me on his lap, I can see him as clearly as I can see you, and he loved me; oh, how he loved me. Well. I was his youngest, he was an old man by the time I was born. May his soul rest in peace, he was some man. In Russia, he owned land, he kept lambs. In Russia. A Jew couldn't own land, but my father had special rights. The Jews in the town, even the Gentiles, they worshiped him. Anytime there was a problem, a husband and wife, two men squabble over a cow, they came to my father. He was like a judge. So. You see where your roots are. He didn't come to this country in steerage."

And a Yiddish lilt crept into her voice, and her eyes grew soft as they saw the past, as if the past were in soft focus, as in a romantic film from the thirties.

She crushed out her cigarette. "And now, look at me. To live in Jackson Lice, Long Island. My father would turn over in his grave."

They'd wooed her together, a team, Ben's father and his uncle Cy. It was Leo Kagan she fell in love with, but it was his brother Cy, Cy "Colburn," who'd made the money, who convinced my mother she was marrying into a "family of Somebodies." She didn't understand that Leo was nothing but Cy's frightened servant. And so she gave up her career.

Frightened servant: how much that leaves out. Trying to tote it all up now, half a century later, he knows his father was more than that: a powerful man, a tender man when he wasn't frightened, a man well loved by the taxi drivers, the fleet owners, the cops, the tire changers he worked with every day. But he couldn't stand up for himself, and when their father became sick, Cy sent him to California—again and again—to nurse the old man. Leo didn't know how to refuse.

And maybe he didn't *want* to. Did he flee from her, using his brother's orders as an excuse? He stayed in California four months, then a year later for nine months, again, six months. Without Leo around to curse for her lot in life, she grew more inward and strange, saw no one, surrendered. Ben was her "reason for living." At night she prowled the house, smoking. He would wake to find her standing in the doorway, watching him sleep.

Last month Ben found this letter among her papers. Not a

carbon. His father must have brought it back with him from California. *If* she ever sent it.

June 10, 1949

Dearest Leo,

Your Thursday letter came today. With the snapshots. Your face looks good, and you don't look too heavy. But your pants need pressing, and don't they wear ties in California?

Please, Leo, don't say to me, "please be sweet." <u>I have been sweet too long</u>. It is now into the sixth month since you went away. That's nice, isn't it? I don't say you went there out of choice, but after all, you are not a dummy, and if you are a human being, you could have said the second month you were there, "I am going home to my wife and child." Well, you are as you are, and I will never change you, Leo.

Enclosed you will find a short letter from Ben. Why he loves you is more than I can say. He is deserving of a devoted father not a dummy who is shoved around by his brother.

I will have to pay Hoover $14.65 for repair Thursday. Remember, Leo, I have been a good wife, and a girl a man doesn't have to be ashamed of. And I have given you all my love, Leo dear. But your staying away has disgusted me beyond repair.

Love,

Myra

When it grew too terrible for her—and by the time Ben was eight it grew too terrible nearly every day—she would stagger to her late-afternoon bitter nap, seasick, grope to bed, holding herself straight by fingering the walls. She slept, then, and woke transformed—back centuries, an ancient Jewish crone. If Leo Kagan was away in California, she stood in the doorway to Ben's room and mumbled curses in Yiddish.

"Mom? What is it?"

She nodded her head rhythmically as if to offer assent, an audience of one, to her own propositions of suffering. She thumped her breast and rocked. Ben wanted him to come home and do something with her, for her. "As God is my judge," she'd say. "You see what my life is?" she'd say—but then she was past rational, saying, *"Mein lieb ist schwartz,* black is my life, black is my blood, *schwartz, schwartz,* my life is black, my blood is black," Yiddish, English, as she rocked. Until she could raise the pitch of pain enough to thump her breast through her nightgown, score bloody claw tracks deep in the skin of her arm, always nails of her left hand into skin of her right arm, and blood would lift in the old places to the surface of her skin.

But it was Ben's father she needed.

When he was back from California, often she'd still be asleep when he came home at night, her late afternoon, early evening stupor. He'd come home and scrub the walls she'd stained with her fingers, or he'd sit at his desk, back turned. There he was, paying a pile of bills, the whole weight of his enormous back and shoulders protesting what she was costing him. She'd wake. She'd stand behind him, holding onto the doorjamb, rocking.

"Sonofabitch, you sonofabitch, oh, you sonofabitch. A Man, some man I married," and Leo's neck thickened and he went down deeper into himself, all that flesh and muscle thickened, hunched against her words.

Until—"GODDAMN you!"—he'd jerk to his feet, maybe knocking over the red velvet bench and making the floor lamp wobble, and that chaos would let him release his rage and he'd bellow, his face flaming, "I've had plenty from you!"

Now she'd have her claws out, pawing the air before her eyes, and the wild old shtetl crone look on her face, lower lip folded down, teeth bared. "Come on, you!" she'd hiss, old Russian Jew Medusa; and, clumsy bear, he'd come at her, she'd scratch out, he'd grab and slap, push her toward the bedroom, and sometimes she'd let him, sometimes she'd moan and go down, crumple to the carpet, tragedy-queen poisoned, eyes rolled back—too slow and too graceful to be completely real.

"Your mother's a crazy woman—I hardly touched her. Get water, Ben."

Or say he yelled at her and didn't touch her, just yelled in his amazing army sergeant voice Ben blocked out with fingers in his ears—then she would forget her original curses, would rush from window to window, shutting, shutting, "so the neighbors shouldn't hear," and so he'd bellow louder, he'd open the goddamn windows after her and *really* yell.

"And *you!* You goddamned mama's boy, you, you spoiled little mama's boy, you're the cause of half the goddamned fights in this house. Money! You think I'm made of money?"—because most of the fights began over money, day after day of one continuous battle about buying and not buying. Battle over his inadequacy to justify her life, her renunciation of the amazing career she'd built for herself, justify becoming a Good Jewish Wife.

Now, when he turned on Ben, she'd stop cursing, smile all of a sudden—"*I'll* tell you what!"—as if she'd just had *such* a clever and amusing idea, smile politely, and rush to the oven, turn on the gas without lighting it and, crawling on her knees, stick her head inside. Then Ben's father would yank her away, shut off the stove, open the window, and wave a dishrag. "You want to blow us all up, you crazy woman?" Or else she'd run to the bathroom and pull open the door to the medicine cabinet, stand deciding which bottle would do the job on her. He'd grab her away. And she'd weep. And he'd lead her, gently, lovingly, to the bedroom, rubbing and patting her bent back, and put her to bed.

When Ben was bar mitzvahed, the fights intensified—she wanted a catered affair at the Pierre. This was, of course, impossible. Half a year's salary. More. Leo put his foot down—if there had to be a bar mitzvah, let it be a simple party upstairs in the social hall of the damned synagogue. She had to settle for that, but it led to the one time she did more than weep or curse or threaten.

She left him.

First, the usual shouting, then theatrical laughter. "I'll tell you what!" Another gesture of suicide? But no—she rushed, hands in front of her as if through a fog, into the bedroom. He went back to his *Journal American,* unfolding it with a furious shake. Half an hour later, snazzy in her good black dress and old Persian lamb coat, suitcase in hand, she came into Ben's room. "Ben, dearest—I'll call you when I'm settled."

"What are you talking about?"

"You see how it is, my dear."

"Mom! Really?"

"Tell that man good-bye."

That man stood in the doorway, arms folded over his chest. "What the hell d'you think you're doing?"

"Nice weather, isn't it? I'll call you when I'm settled."

"You can go to hell for all I care."

"Sweet," she said. Taking up her suitcase, she walked out the front door.

"She'll be back," he said. "Where's she gonna find a cab at this hour?"

"I'll follow her."

"You will not follow her. She'll be back in five minutes if you don't make a big fuss. Crazy person. Where's she gonna go?"

He went back to his paper. Ben listened for the elevator but hoped he wouldn't hear it. He felt giddy with this gesture, its possibilities.

"What's she doing, goddamn woman," he said after a few minutes. "Walking the streets!" He folded his glasses neatly into their case, put on his coat and trudged out. "Stay put in case she calls. She's probably—you know where?—standing right down-stairs."

But he didn't come back—half an hour he didn't come back. Then the telephone rang.

"Hello, my darling son."

"Where *are* you?"

"Is he there?"

"He's out looking for you."

"The poor fool. I'm registered at the Plaza."

"The Plaza? The Plaza on Fifty-ninth?"

"There's only one Plaza, my dear."

"Well, what are you doing at the Plaza?"

"I'm not quite sure," she said after a moment. "Perhaps I'm teaching him a lesson."

"Maybe," Ben said, "you ought to stay away for a while. Maybe—Mom?—you ought to get back into business? Mom? Why not get back into business, call Mr. Bonwit. Why not?"

"You think I couldn't?"

"I didn't say you couldn't. Maybe you'd be better off is what I said. Maybe you'd be much better off, Mom."

"What would your poor father do without me?"

Ben listened to the hiss of the wires. He listened to his mother breathing. Neither of them spoke for a long time. "Mom? You want him to call you?"

"Let him worry," she said. "But tomorrow, if *you* wish to visit your mother . . . "

How could he keep it a secret? She must have known, he thinks now, fifty years after that night. After they hung up, he left a note for his father and went downstairs after him. But he was nowhere—not the drugstore on the corner, the subway station. He must be out hunting for her in the car.

A taxi swung around the corner. If it hadn't happened along, he would have gone back home to wait, but, without thinking, he flagged it down. "To the Plaza Hotel," he said, and felt in the name the magic she felt.

As they crossed the East River, he ignored the lights of the city, kept his eye on the meter, and fingered the loose bills and change—pay and tips from delivering for the drugstore. It was just fifteen minutes to the hotel, grand chateau with its green mansard roof lit up, and inside, mirrors and candelabra brilliant after the dark ride.

"Mrs. Kagan?" Ben asked at the desk. "She's my mother—she just registered."

There was no Mrs. Kagan. Panic caved him in, what was he doing at the Plaza Hotel in the middle of the night? Didn't he know better than to believe her? But then he asked, "What about Bresloff? Myra Bresloff?"

The desk clerk nodded, finger over some list. "Miss Bresloff? Room 414."

"In case anybody calls," Ben said, "it's the same person. Miss Bresloff, Mrs. Kagan. Bresloff is her business name. It's the same person."

Her room faced the park—nothing but the best. She was still in her black dress. "Well, isn't this a surprise." Ben looked around. The windows looked out on the lamps of Central Park. Dirty windows and paint peeling from the corner moldings and the carpets were sad, for the Plaza hadn't yet been restored.

"It's come down in the world," she said. "But it's a little bit of all right. It's still the Plaza." She looked her son over. "Couldn't you dress up a little? That old shirt of yours—"

"Who *cares?* Mom, what are you doing? Are you really leaving him?"

"Don't I deserve a vacation?"

"You deserve. Oh, *sure* you deserve..." Taking in everything, he noticed her beautiful suitcase from the old days, with its brass fittings and fine linen sides covered by pale fleur-de-lis. It sat on a luggage rack for the maid to admire.

"That's some workmanship, isn't it?" she said. "You see the

workmanship? You should have heard me *hondel* with the salesman. This was many years ago of course. When do I go anywhere
these days?" she sighed. "This is for your wife someday, after I'm
gone."

She watched him looking at the high filigree ceiling.

"Long before you were born—this is as true as I'm standing
here—I was at a party for Al Jolson at the Plaza. Naturally, it was
the finest suite in the hotel. Everybody in New York was there—"

"*That,*" Ben said, "must have been some suite."

"Smart. Jolson and I talked about family. At heart what was
he, after all, but a good, simple, Jewish boy?"

The telephone. Ben's father. She listened.

"*No,* my dear," she said finally. "I'm not *coming* home."
Hanging up on him, she turned to me. "He won't let me alone.
Well, naturally. . . . Would you like anything from room service?"

"Where did you get the money?" Ben asked.

"Well, and shouldn't a woman keep a little money in her
own name?"

"I'm not *blaming* you, Mom." Ben stared out at the lights of
cars cruising the perimeter road in Central Park.

"If you were a little older, I could tell you a few things."

A light tap at the door. Suddenly, Ben understood: his call
must have come not from home but from downstairs. And she
must have known this already, but she went to the door as if
curious.

"Myra."

"Hmmm," she said, hand on her hip. "You've had enough?"

"Listen, you've been crazy enough for one night. Would you
get your bag?"

"My dear—"

"Oh, don't give me that phony voice, Myra. For godsakes."

"Isn't he elegant, Ben?" And then, all of a sudden, like turning off an electric light, her face dissolved, the gracious lady dissolved, she grimaced as if pain had caught her heart, as if she were

choking, and she shook her head. "Yah. Yah. Yah. Nice. Elegant. You think this is a joke? It's no joke. My life isn't a joke. Understand?"

She sank into a big armchair, and he, not asking nor being prevented, collected her things and snapped the fancy suitcase shut. Then, not speaking to her, he lifted her, unresisting, half-limp, from the chair. "Come on. We're going home. Ben, take her coat."

They hardly talked on the way. Home, still she didn't talk. Except to moan, "This is some life. Look at this life. Jackson Lice." And he said, "Leave us alone for a while, will you, Ben?" From the closed bedroom there was no shouting—just thick, guttural whispers.

Ben tried finishing his homework, but as his eyes read, his ears listened. Whispers answering whispers. "Then we can move," he heard his father say aloud. Then whispers. Waiting for it to be over, Ben brewed a cup of tea and sat in the kitchen, remains of a pot roast still in the platter, cold grease caked around the brown meat. Then weeping. He drank his tea. When the door opened and footsteps came and went, he stood at the end of the hall and looked into the bedroom. She was sitting beside him, rubbing his back, and *he* was the one crying, his big father crying, and she was saying, "You are what you are, my dear." Then, to Ben—"You know how I love your father."

This love, that seemed to take away her life. Ben never understood this love, as years later, when he was himself married, he couldn't understand her telephone call.

"My *son?*"

It was the vibrato in her voice that let him know his father was dead. "It's Dad?"

"One hour ago. A heart attack—you know what his heart was like. I had to collect myself to call you. 'Myra,' he said to me as if he had a joke to tell. Then he took a step toward me and he fell like a tree. Like a tree. Poor soul. Poor simple soul."

"I'm very sorry, Mom."

"God grants some special people very gentle deaths. He was dead, your father, before he touched the floor, so he wouldn't feel the hurt from the fall. I turned him onto his back myself—he was light as a feather. You know the weight he lost. So. So. So. It's done. It's finished. *Fertig*. A life. You understand me? No. How can you? That man—he was as good as gold to me."

"Good to you?"

"A better man God never made."

"Mom. I'll be down in the morning. You'll be all right tonight?"

"Listen, my dear—you have a decent suit?"

The photographs on Ben's staircase walls were culled out of the boxes his mother left when she died. Whatever happened to her suitcase with the fleur-de-lis? Was it stolen along with the blue willow? At least there were these photographs going back, back through the forties, the thirties, the twenties, the war, to Russia. His father, born in Odessa, Ukraine, then Russia, 1894; his mother in Kishnief, Bessarabia, then Russia, 1904. His mother, his father, coming so far from Russia to marry in New York, coming all that way as if God had laid out a plan, a mystical conjunction, so that they could live with one another in love and misery.

Highest up the stairs is a photo of his mother in the late twenties, her own midtwenties, another world, before she married. Fur wrap over wool suit, she stands on a deck of a ship—porthole, brass fittings, polished wood—with a friend, *"with the wonderful actress Joyce Bancroft"* written floridly at the bottom of the photograph. Both of them hamming it up for the camera. Playing elegant. He remembers the posture. So young they seem. He could be their father. He could offer her advice. Knowing that in just a few years she will meet the man on the other side of the stairs, that good-looking, overweight man posing with baseball bat as if waiting for a pitch, grinning with all his powerful good nature for the camera. A man with drinking buddies. Scared of women. Loyal to his parents. Scared of taking chances. He will do well enough early through his charm, then pale, fade, work in fear and loyalty and trust for his brother, love a woman who was too much for him, too complicated, too smart, too full of the need to be grand, love a woman he had nothing in common with *except* love, then retire to grumpiness and heart attack.

But there he is, pretending confidence, waiting for the pitch, and across the stairs, she has her eye on him.

# Open-Heart Surgery

*O*n the operating table, as the cocktail of anesthetics took effect, Ned Koenig felt paralyzed before he was unconscious. He was not breathing but being breathed. He wasn't really *there* anymore—a machine functioned in his place, and he was attached to this machine, *being lived*.

This wasn't a totally unfamiliar experience.

His heart must have known the pain of having to live another day and another, year after year of having to perform for others— for *an* other, who was himself—until, one day, it balked like a horse at its thousandth jump. Flying back to Boston from L.A., he grew weak, then dizzy, and lugging his overnight bag to a taxi wondered was it down his arm, was it in his chest, those pains? He was sweating in the tunnel, maybe from embarrassment that he was going to have to ask the driver to take him to emergency at Mass General.

Leaning into the car to take his change, he must have passed out, for he found himself splayed on the sidewalk with money in his hand and the driver (shouting, shrill, frantic, in Hindi or Persian) hurrying out of the cab. But he rested a moment and was up, attaché case in hand, followed by the cabdriver with his suitcase. He didn't let himself crumple until he'd reached the desk and gotten his Blue Cross card out of his wallet.

This was characteristic of Koenig. It was his greatest satisfaction, to complete a project. He was a well-respected consultant in direct mail and telemarketing, highly paid—so outlandishly paid that his income surpassed that of most of the CEOs he dealt with. He *got the work done*—that's what mattered to him. It disturbed him to talk to people whose deepest satisfaction lay in exhibiting themselves, in getting petted, in telling you how powerful they were, in scoring, in shining. Koenig was interested in the work, that six-in-the-morning he could be up with coffee in front of his terminal, captain of the ship—with Margaret (if she happened to be home, for they both traveled) still asleep, the dog asleep, a Haydn trio coming in over his headphones—creating the shape of the program that might turn around sales for another company:

- Methodically dividing the problem into its parts as company thinking conceived it;
- Making an imaginative leap that bypassed the original blockage, the stuck-place, because if there was a solution (and sometimes there was none except to dissolve the company), there was always something stuck in the company's thinking.

Once he found the stuck-place, he could feel his own thinking open itself to light and his words be moved by that light into the shape of the report. He'd wait until they had accepted the report, and then he'd fly back to Dallas or Atlanta or Los Angeles to show them how to implement the plan of action.

His body, after the attack, he saw as a company in trouble. This time, he was the one who had to call in a consultant.

Acute myocardial infarction. He rested a week; the company could function again. But the consultants made it clear: he would need a double coronary bypass.

Koenig was sensible, always. Facing a problem, he grew calm. If you needed a team to blow up a bridge, you'd want Koenig. It was a trick, his calm strength, a trick of deliberate detachment, deliberate slowing down. He knew he had none of the inner strength he was given credit for. What *was* inner strength? He'd learned at least that no one could know what was really going on inside; all he had to do was to speak carefully, to smile an assured smile, and other people entered his calm and felt it as strength and took strength from it. That, he supposed, was strength enough.

And so, he let himself be scheduled for surgery. Wanting to avoid what they called "complications," he had his own blood drawn for autologous donation; he let his wife, Margaret, take care of things or, when she had to be away, hire someone to take care of things. He limited his hours at the computer and on the phone; until surgery, he let his equipment rest.

Then he gave it into the hands of professionals, and they wheeled it down corridors, while Koenig watched the ceiling turn at right angles and wondered if he might be about to die. He was only in his late fifties—the percentages were with him—but just in case, his papers were in order, a checklist drawn up on his desk. His son and daughter from his first marriage were grown up, Pete, Lisa; his will provided for them and provided for Margaret, though none of them really needed provision.

The tranquilizer was taking over, and it was nice to let his body go, not to make it get on planes and get off planes, not to chastize it for soreness or flu when he needed it working well if the job was going to get done. He felt a little giddy with relief from all that. Separation from the machine was familiar enough, but this time he could—he had no choice—not *make it go* but let it go its own way. And then the slow workings of the anesthetic, and then the complete loss of his responsibility for the distant body, and then the surge of his own breath, his own heart thumping in his ears, and pain, pain, just under the medication.

After all, they'd split him in half like a broiler, sawed through his ribs and come inside. They'd removed a vein from his thigh, and from beneath his nipple plucked that strange female anomaly in a man, his internal mammary artery, and had somehow spliced them both in, in place of the occluded passages. It was amazing to him that a day later they had him out of bed and walking a little. In just over a week he was home and the children could fly back to their lives and Margaret to a business meeting, though she was home the next day to take walks with him around the yard, then down the street and back.

"I think you enjoy me helpless," he kidded her.

"When else do I have a chance to take care of you?"

It was a good second marriage. She chose him, he suspected, partly because he let her rest from her competence. Sometimes she liked—this intense woman of business—to pretend to be frail and frivolous and let him be the *doer*. Now, he rested, and she *did*.

It was in his music he found the first strangeness.

Leaning back on his pillows, skimming the *Globe,* only half listening to whatever cassette he'd inserted in the Walkman, he realized that he was suffused with the music, that he was taking it in through his heart, as if it were an organ of perception instead of a muscle. This wasn't his metaphorical heart but something at his chest that was taking the music inside and diffusing it through his body in waves of—not exactly color, but something very like. Even becoming self-conscious didn't stop the process, though it did stop the instant he tried to *hear* the music, a quartet by Brahms—to hear the old way: *through his ears.* Then he wanted to hear in the new way and for a moment panicked—he'd forgotten *how!* But oh, there it was again, absorbed into his chest and vibrating. The sound, of course, entered his ears still, but the *music* came in at the chest. His whole body was weak with music, like after making love.

When he tried to listen, turning his eyes up to hear better, it dissolved. There was in fact new clarity of attention when he listened with his ears, but there wasn't—as when he dropped his eyes and opened his chest—that same music at the heart making his face wet with tears. *The medications,* he thought, but there was only a painkiller at night, and, when he felt the need, a low dose of tranquilizer, nothing he hadn't taken before. In his mind's eye he opened his chest as if the ribs, having been split open, knew the way now to peel themselves back and let the music in.

Fearing to lose it, he didn't tell Margaret. Evenings, he sat with her while she worked on a report, and he listened. It was like having in the music a secret lover. But at the same time, it brought him closer to her.

He'd met Margaret through music, was charmed by her first because of the way she looked playing violin in a string quartet, a serious amateur group she still played with, though less and less so as each of the players grew more successful, more immersed in their careers. His early weekends with Margaret were built around concerts; the summer they married, they took a place near Marlboro, Vermont, during the chamber music festival. And still, once in a while, they went to concerts together. But as time passed they began to keep more each to themselves, he working in his study, she in hers. Fewer evenings, they had sat with sherry listening together in their living room.

It was a high-ceilinged room, warm, with ornate moldings and built-in bookcases (but who had time to read?), a soft taupe wall-to-wall carpet and lush fabrics, afghans and cashmere throws draped over the velvet arms of sofa and chairs and antimacassars. Margaret filled it with flowers that wilted when they were away. The room made his son, Pete, laugh—it was so Viennese, so, well, *uncool.* Koenig didn't care. And they weren't ashamed to have it full of photos. Margaret was kind to his photos from before they met. He was kind to her old books. He and Margaret would tell each other over the phone (he in San Diego, she in Denver), *We really ought to spend more time in the living room together just listening.*

They made it a point. Last year, her fiftieth birthday, he'd given her a fine violin from the early nineteenth century, a Gabriel Lennbock, and she'd cried and held it to her breast like a living creature—though rarely did she have time to practice. But when they sat together in the evening, she'd take it out and play an old piece for him, something she'd worked up for a recital thirty-five years ago. He wondered whether she always heard as he was hearing now, with her heart. He was embarrassed to ask.

So it wasn't that he had never loved music—for he had, always. But now he went back to his CDs and cassettes with his mouth open and jolts of anxiety at his diaphragm in anticipation of what would happen to him as the old music entered his new organ.

Nothing to worry about, certainly nothing to talk to Dr. Cogswell about. Still, he wondered: was it just the new lease on life and all this untoward rest—or was it some peculiarity of the operation? He imagined someone deaf to all but middle frequencies his entire life who then had an operation changing that—to hear so much, to hear music fully, must be dizzying. *This* was dizzying.

He was back at work, first at home, soon at a company in New Hampshire—he could drive up and back. And then one morning, after less than two months, he was flying to Los Angeles again. Margaret was concerned, but Koenig was eager. He could see his son on the way out. He arranged a stopover at O'Hare.

These past few years, it was mostly at airports that he saw Pete (Chicago) and Lisa (San Francisco). Five, six times a year, Koenig, a little ragged, but cheerful, waving, came into the peculiar combination of fluorescence and sunlight of an airport lounge, and he and Pete ceremonially hugged and patted, or he and Lisa hugged and didn't pat, and Pete took up his overnight bag or Lisa his attaché case, and they walked to the airline club for lunch or a drink. It was just enough time to catch up and not enough for silences to brew. They showed each other photos, they recited successes. Pete was doing corporate law, Lisa was assistant curator at a museum and finishing a doctorate in art history at Berkeley. She was engaged, Pete was "seeing people." Koenig was pleased with both his children. He loved them, would have died for them. But as the years passed, he knew them less and less; maybe he knew his tennis partners better. It was sad, it was what happened to parents and children. Yet they flew to be with him for his surgery. And after, embracing him clumsily, they were haggard, they had cried. Their outpouring of plans and memories seemed foreign to him.

Maybe it was that. Still, he hadn't anticipated this meeting, not even as he waved to Pete at O'Hare. This time, Koenig wasn't smiling as he came up the dark tube into the airport lobby. He was frightened and didn't know whether he ought to tell Pete, *Something happened in the plane to me.* . . .

In the plane:

It might have been the five milligrams of Valium or anxiety about getting back to his life. But he suspected it was something that went wrong in the operation, a miswiring; maybe too much blood was flowing, and his brain couldn't handle it.

He'd settled himself, headphones on, to let his heart apprehend a quartet by Beethoven. He sat, eyes half-shut, through the takeoff and climb; then, at cruising altitude he looked out at the quilted farmland and woodland and the little towns of western Massachusetts, and found himself *seeing* with his heart.

*Oh my God,* he whispered through the music. At this great distance, five miles high, it wasn't frightening. He was scarcely in a plane at all. He let the land below flow into his open chest and dissipate through his blood to make his feet and fingers hum. The light was, of course, still entering at his eyes; it was, he supposed, just a diffused form of seeing that let him absorb all at once the web of relations—texture, color, shape. (He'd call Dr. Cogswell as soon as he was back.)

Then, filled with the land below, he rubbed his eyes and turned to the interior of the plane. He started up the aisle toward the bathroom at the rear, and suddenly, looking at the passengers, he was taken up, the way it must be in labor, the first strong contractions carrying a woman with them past control. There was no control. He was invaded, and it wasn't like music, it wasn't like landscape. *Cogswell had done this!* There were all these lives entering his chest, faces of desire mixing inside him, and he grew frantic and turned back to his seat, shrank back with his eyes closed to feel his heart's new beat. And he knew his calm had been a way of keeping things out, keeping the other in its own separate place, keeping it for his use, and nothing could do that now.

What was so terrible? Eyes closed, he thought, *I'm simply not used to it. Relax. It's just people's lives, or my own feelings I'm putting on them.* But he didn't have the courage to look again, and when the plane landed in Chicago, he kept his eyes lowered. His heart was open to the energy of legs and hands, briefcases of money-hunger, dark blue business suits of aggression. He felt erotic tumult like the time he'd taken a nephew to a water slide and got shamed into going along, got water up his nose and a stiff neck trying to fight the slide, and still the only way was to let go; then it was almost all right, he gave himself to the fall and sank and sank, rising to his nephew's laughter.

And then he saw Pete at the gate, something to hold on to in all this, and he waved. Pete took his case and said, "Should you be carrying something that heavy? Jesus—what've you got in here? Good to see you up again, Dad."

"Something's been happening to me," Koenig began, and then he looked Pete in the eyes and couldn't keep him out, his heart saw, and his heart was open-mouthed and voracious, his heart couldn't keep decent boundaries, and Ned Koenig began to sob, and Pete was saying, "Come on, we'll get to the TWA club room, it's okay, you've been through something." And Ned Koenig tried to say to his son, "No, it's *now* I'm going through something," but his son was patting his shoulder, telling stories, covering over, saying, "You hungry, Dad? What's your food trip post-op? Low cholesterol and what else?" But Ned was without defenses: he was taking in this son he loved so much, infant he'd snuggled naked and little boy he'd held against rough waves how many summers, youth he'd shored up and backed away from and pushed out as surely as if he were birthing him a second time, then mourned his loss, only he wasn't lost, he was impossibly, unbearably present, flesh of his flesh. Now, seeing Pete through tears, Ned felt Pete's own loss, that Pete had become like his father, had learned his father's tricks, and while Ned wished he could use those tricks again, he felt the sham, and couldn't stand it when he felt this close to this son and knew his son was using them.

Pete was ordering for both of them; he was asking about the consultation in L.A., about Margaret, about the stitches, finally about these peculiar feelings his dad was having and "Have you . . . seen somebody, a doctor, maybe some short-term therapy—Dad, everyone is looking."

Ned reached out to touch his son's face, but this was much worse than sound or sight—*touch* knocking at his heart. He drew back his fingers; he could see Pete withdraw his eyes until they were camera lenses, not eyes anymore.

*"Please, Dad!"*

Ned was weeping for both of them.

And then he was running up an incline toward the terminal, running from his son. "Dad," Pete called in pursuit over boarding announcement, howling child, "all I said was, you ought to think about checking into a hospital. You're not ready for business, not like this."

But Ned Koenig was running, overnight bag in one hand, attaché case in the other, and Pete was running after. Arriving passengers flooding from a gate got between them.

"Dad! You can't run like that. You *can't*."

Koenig stopped and called back, "Then don't run after me, Pete. You don't run, I won't run."

"Okay. Okay. Please. I'm not moving, Dad."

"Here. I'm leaving the bag." The terminal's great fluorescent space swallowed his voice; they were only twenty yards, a scattering of people, apart, but he had to shout. "I'm buying a ticket home." He left his heavy bag and slipped into the crowd.

He took the next flight back to Boston, first class; Margaret was at Logan to meet him—he knew what that must have cost her, busy as she was. He wanted to comfort her but was afraid what might happen should he touch her hand or look her in the face. He was in disarray, hand-tailored Italian suit crumpled and Mark Cross necktie slack. It must look as if he were a lush and his elegant wife were picking up the pieces.

"I made an appointment with Dr. Cogswell. Pete says you think they made a *mistake* in the operation. A mistake? Why don't you look at me, Ned? Ned? What kind of mistake?"

He looked at her, and with no chest to protect him how could he keep her out? She wasn't the handsome, ironic woman who'd attended concerts with him, who shared with him the same financial planner; the woman who, when they both happened to be in Boston, made love with him in the dark before sleep, then laughed and kissed his nose, his chin, his cheek. She entered him now as flame without heat, there was nothing else but this fire. The terror wasn't that she was someone strange, a foreign body, but that, entering at the heart this way and filling him, she wouldn't leave any room for *him*.

He wrapped himself in his own arms and turned from her, like the Virgin from the angel, terrified to bear this annunciation. But she had her arm around him, and her touch rushed through him like a hot wind.

*"It's all right, Ned. I'll get you home. We'll see the doctor."*

She was soothing him, afraid for him. He wanted to say, "Cogswell has to fix this," but now he knew there was no repair. His body wasn't separate from himself, a set of problems to solve. Even though his mouth was agape with terror, his heart, full of world, was unwilling to return to its safe separation. Willing himself not to fight, he took both her hands and then his heart was suffused with light that lived through him. He was only a vehicle being lived by the light, until, tossed by the tumult, he was flooded at the heart with light that was almost pain. Light was all there was and all there would ever be.

# Dance to the Old Words

*O*nly one year of separation, but look how much his children had already taught him. For the first six months, Eli, five years old, then six, would cry at night, middle of *every* night, and Jake would have to lie down with him, pressed firmly against his back like a lover. Next morning, Eli didn't remember. And not just that he didn't remember: you couldn't believe this was the same creature who'd wept so hard, who was barely in the shared world, barely aware of his father's comfort. Often, those first months Jake held him the way he had when Eli was two.

It was getting better for Eli now. Jake loved the brave way Eli would hold up his skinny frame, like a knight, and breathe to fill his chest with grown-up-ness. But Sebastian, at eleven, was still often furious and unforgiving. When he wasn't storming, he was sullen, storing up grievances. Jake learned to respect Sebastian's silences but to hold firm.

This morning, as he caught one of Sebastian's sour looks —they were hustling to get him to his soccer game—Jake held

Sebastian by the shoulders. "Look—we've done you damage, and it's lousy, it's not fair, and that's what you're saying with those crappy looks of yours. Right?"

"No, it's not. But it stinks, it *does stink,* if you want to know."

"All right, so it stinks. But I won't be guilt-tripped. You can yell at me or punch a pillow, that's okay, Sebastian, but when you're finished, you've still got to set the table and keep your things in order and get to bed at a reasonable hour and be ready on time in the morning."

All the mad precision of scheduling to keep the children on an even keel while they lived in one house for a week, then the other for a week—was absolutely required to turn a mess into a reasonable life. It was fucking exhausting. But there was no good option. Children were conservative creatures, nurtured best in habit and ritual; even predictable oppression was better than chaos. Chaos was the alternative, the enemy, chaos was the real devil.

"Let's get out to the field," Jake said. "You want hot cereal?"

Sebastian's eyes softened. "Eggs. Okay?" He had such deep, soulful eyes, Jake thought; he imagined him as a young man looking into the eyes of a friend. Grateful for the softening, he found his own eyes welling up.

"Sunny-side, coming up," he said in his short-order voice.

"This has been a tough time for husbands and fathers," Jake began one of his articles. "They're seen as large, clumsy beasts that need to be domesticated. Valuable for fixing electric wiring but resented for somehow keeping a monopoly on such knowledge. Resented for keeping emotionally distant from their family; resented, too, for emotionally intruding. They're seen as dangerous to women and children."

Jake, on the other hand, believed in a child's need for a father who could help establish the moral parameters, the ground rules, who gave a child a firm structure to push off against. Not that he saw himself as this model father; but he felt he knew what was at stake.

At gentle heat he cooked up eggs for the three of them. Hell with my cholesterol. Toast from his own baked bread. Sebastian had settled down. He laced up his cleats and told them how fast and slippery the Cambodian center on the other team was rumored to be.

Jake sat high above the field in the wooden bleachers. All the fathers, a couple of mothers, hunched up in parkas on this cold, gray Saturday. Jake had his eye on one of the mothers, a single mom he'd spoken to a couple of times. Thickening in torso, curly hair turning gray, Jake saw himself as still a handsome man, maybe on the rough side but handsome; he never had a problem getting women to want him. The problem was how to fit new women into his life with work and kids. Or was that just a cover? On second thought, maybe this new woman was a bad idea right now.

Sebastian took the ball down on wing; Eli hunkered against his father, yelling, "Come on, Sebi! Sebi! Yes!"

A whistle for the half. No score.

Now a strange thing: a man by the players' bench waved at Sebastian, and Sebastian waved back. Eli poked Jake. "Dad! Daddy! That man there, it's *Carl*, Mom said not to talk to him. *Can* I talk to him?" He ran down the stands between the fathers. "Carl, Carl!"

A couple of months ago, Jake would have been pissed. This guy invading my turf! Confusing my kids. Screw him! It was different now. Christine had dumped Carl, too. Just as with Jake himself—no warning, she made the decision, that was that. "Ha! Y'see?" Jake gloated. "She dumps everybody."

So when Carl climbed the stands, Eli trailing, Jake grinned at him as if they shared a joke. Carl looked uneasy, wanting permission. "You're Jake Peretz. Sebastian and Eli's father—I've seen your picture. I'm Carl Degler. I've been wanting to meet you." Lean, nice-looking, red-haired, Degler was dressed in an elegant suede belted jacket and suede boots and fine corduroy slacks—

casual clothes that must have cost near a thousand bucks. He was a few years younger and looked younger still. Jake held out his hand. "Have some coffee?" Jake found a styrofoam cup and poured.

Jake is a Jew. He hears a name like Carl Degler? Probably an anti-Semite. His kids brought up by an anti-Semite! Country house and BMW he knew about; the rest he made up. Christine told him that Degler bought software and medical technology in Eastern Europe. Jake turned him into a ruthless business type, maybe trading in weapons, maybe hiring nuclear scientists for Iran.

So now he was giggling because that sinister Nazi wheeler-dealer in the BMW had turned into a prep-school type who spoke in complete sentences, precisely, with no expressive edge. "I've read quite a number of your articles in the *Nation*," Degler said. Jake was always listening for language. He was aware that, talking to Degler, he himself was speaking *Brooklyn,* the Brooklyn of his childhood, exploding the stressed syllables, hitting the dentals hard, pumping up the city beat of his sentences. Hostile?—i.e., street-smart, populist, hip, against Connecticut prep-school *politesse?* Yeah, maybe hostile—but expressive, too, of male comradery. One-on-one.

Maybe the mix of his father and his mother's ex-boyfriend confused Eli. "Dad, I'm going down to the field, okay, Dad?"

As Eli danced off, Degler said, "They always talked about you."

Jake shrugged off the gift. "Yeah. Well, I'm not letting go. I'll hang on with my teeth like a fucking pit bull."

"I came here to say good-bye," Degler said. "Christine won't let me near them."

"I know. She told me." Jake guffawed—but shook his head in sympathy.

After the game—someone on Sebastian's team ricocheted a last-minute goal off someone's shins—the two teams lined up and passed one another, shaking hands. Jake had an idea. "Hey, Carl—why don't you come back with us, have cold cuts back at my place? Yeah, yeah, it's all right. It's *my place*. You ought to be able to say good-bye, for chrissakes. It's only right."

The boys walked together in front. Jake caught a glimpse of Sebastian's solemn face and could read his subdued excitement. "That Cambodian kid was good, but you guys, ha!—you took them to the cleaners," Jake called out, and Sebastian turned and grinned. Eli was blabbing, high-pitched, dramatic; he danced a soccer ball down the path to the cars.

Digging through the refrigerator, he called out, "Sebastian, Eli, I want you guys to go pack, and straighten up your rooms, you're leaving at five. I'll get lunch on the table. Checklists are on your desks." He opened bags of cold cuts. He saw Degler look the place over as if trying to find something nice to say.

It was a beat-up old kitchen, nothing like the new kitchen in the house he'd had to leave a year ago. He did the work himself to keep costs down—took a sledgehammer to the old plaster walls and in rage and pleasure pulled the lathing until all his muscles ached and his throat was full of dust. He only griped once in a while, but he had to admit it was a come-down to this rented place. Here he was, still paying half the mortgage for that beautiful old Newton house while he had to live here like a student.

The furniture he took was the old stuff that came to him from his parents or from his first marriage. Old sofa that had weathered two marriages—the new sofa, Christine held on to. Well, he didn't want to change the home the boys were used to. So for himself he bought used tables and chairs. The scratched, white enameled kitchen table was just like one his mother had stored away when he was a kid. It embarrassed him a little, bringing Degler to a place like this. But he loved sticking it to Christine. It would bust her balls!

With the boys away getting packed, Jake and Carl fell silent.

"Can I get you a beer? You probably think this is typical—cold cuts, I mean," Jake said. "I don't know what she told you."

"Actually, she said you were a good cook."

"I *like* cooking, anyway. Last night I made 'Adventurers Stew'—that's actually *boeuf Bourguignon*, but don't tell the kids. And you?" Jake asked Degler. "You have any children?"

"No. I was married to a businesswoman," he said, as if that explained something. Then Degler wandered off. And after a while Jake, making up a pitcher of lemonade at the sink, overheard him talking to Sebastian and Eli. "Just so you understand—I want you to understand. I've really cared about you both. I'll always feel love for you, for both of you. Just so you know. . . . I regret so much the way things worked out. Just so you know. . . ."

"Sure. Thanks," Sebastian said. "Mom gets real mad sometimes."

That was when Jake's heart opened. Until that moment, Carl Degler had been a decent, if white-bread, guy, and the meeting had been a joke on Christine. A *men's* joke. The Guys, teamed up against Women for an afternoon. A confirmation of blamelessness—ahh, who could figure that bitch? But standing at the old, stained, white porcelain sink, squeezing lemon halves into a pitcher, even with the water running Jake could hear Carl's stammering pain, and instantly, the situation became something else, something sadder.

Now, without asking again, Jake opened a beer for Carl and carried it in and handed it to him. Without a word Carl followed him back into the kitchen. Jake laid out the cold cuts on a platter. "A real kick in the stomach for you, huh?"

Carl didn't pretend not to understand. "A *real* kick in the stomach. I didn't expect it. You read about men, they get so obsessed with a woman they go to restaurants on the off chance she'll be there. They haunt the neighborhood. But you see, ordinarily, I'm a pretty conservative person. I never imagined."

"I didn't know—I mean, that it was that bad."

"She actually took out a restraining order."

"I didn't know."

"I'm embarrassed, to be so foolish. And—well, I'm not the type to hurt anyone," Carl said, hands open to show they were clean and safe for children. "But I can imagine it looked bad, my hanging around. I couldn't think of anything else to do. Then I wanted at least to say good-bye to the boys."

"I'm sorry. Sebastian's right. She's one angry woman."

"Sure. Christine's angry, it's true," Carl said. "*Oh. But.* She can be a wonderful, generous woman, too," Carl said. "I know it's a funny thing to say—I never met a woman so splendid."

Jake laughed. "*Splendid,* sure. Splendid I won't deny. I remember a few summers back, a cocktail party in Wellfleet, I look up to see Christine in a long, white summer dress, her skin all tan and her hair loose, lightened gorgeous by the sun, and all around her a circle of these big shots in thrall—professors and analysts and CEOs—she shone like some kind of goddess. It made me hold my goddamned breath. '*I'm* married to *her?*' I said. Soon I wasn't."

"It's funny," Carl said. "She used to tell me how *different* I was from you—I knew her better in a few months than you in ten years. I looked at your picture over Sebastian's bed. I looked up your articles in different magazines. I felt good, being able to take care of her better than you. By the summer, she said I was just like you after all. 'Another arrogant male. Selfish, inconsiderate, controlling.'"

"What is it about Christine?" Jake said. He meant it rhetorically, like, *What's* with *that woman?* But Carl Degler took it as a straight question.

"I think I know," Carl said, "what Christine had for *me.* A long time now, I've been a success in my work, and *in* my work I've felt expansive—you know? I don't put limits on myself. But in my emotional life—a lot of the time I live in a box under brown glass."

"She helped you feel free?"

"She gave me the sense that I *built* the box. I screwed the thing together, you understand? So then maybe, *maybe,* I can dismantle it and walk away."

"But not without Christine, am I right?"

Degler didn't answer. He sipped his beer. The two of them sat at the kitchen table, and Jake began to see something peculiar, to see middle age peel away from Carl Degler; he began to see him the way he must have been twenty years ago. He stared. He didn't want to be rude, but there was something—and he said, "I think I know you. I know you from somewhere."

"You know me? . . . Have you done any articles on the Young Presidents Organization?"

"Who? Me? Are you kidding? No, no—*long ago.* It's something personal. Wait a minute—*you have a sister*—am I right?"

"You know Jenny?"

"*Jenny.* That's right, *Jenny.* But . . . not Jenny Degler."

"No. She's a half sister. Jennifer Corcoran."

"Jenny Corcoran! Sure, I was *with* her for a while. A few months. You used to visit sometimes. That's it."

"The farm! The commune in Vermont."

"Half-Acre Farm. It was a joke, the name. Remember? I lived up there. We lived up there."

"Oh, my God—of course. *Jake.* You lived with Jenny. You played guitar. Right? I'm not sure I ever knew your last name. *Jake.* Sure."

"You came up on weekends."

"You played folk guitar."

From the other room, noises of Nintendo violence. Ordinarily, Jake would have stopped daytime TV, not to mention video games of male violence, and especially when the boys were supposed to be packing. But now he sat grinning at Carl Degler. And Carl smiled back. And then they were laughing and a little too shy to look at one another, and it was like the old days, being stoned and knowing more than you usually let on you know, not censoring it out. Laughing—and finally it was Jake who said it. "Okay, okay. You slept with my wife, I slept with your sister. So—how *is* she, your sister? Hey—I really *liked* her."

"She's good. Married. She has a boy and a girl. She's a lawyer in Denver."

"I'm glad. See? I should have stuck with her." Jake grunted. "But should she have stuck with me? That's a whole other question. And the answer is, fuck, no. I was a wild-ass punk, acting out like crazy."

"Well, it was the times, Jake."

"Naw. I refuse to get off the hook that easy." Jake sighed. "The times just let us be the arrogant pricks we wanted to be."

"But Jenny, too," Carl said. "Her first marriage, she wound up in a terrible depression. . . . Jenny's been through things."

"I'm sorry. She was really fine." Now, as Jake walked into the living room, he remembered her red hair, like her brother's, only so long!—remembered it loose—like sea wrack, he thought, under him in bed, and he imagined a whole other life he hadn't had with Jenny. He couldn't even remember why they stopped being together.

Now, back in the world he was actually living, he shrugged at the boys, palms up (like Carl, he thought)—as if saying, What's this daytime Nintendo crap? "Lunch, you guys." Sebastian shrugged back, got out of the game and called "Eli?" and they came into the kitchen.

And while the boys set the table, Jake poked through his old records and pulled out *American Beauty* by the Grateful Dead. He switched on the small kitchen speakers he'd wired up. It was music he hadn't played for a long, long time. But he was certain that when he sat down at the table, Carl would be nodding to the rhythm of the Dead. And Carl *was*.

Jake thumbed at the music. "I never listen to that stuff anymore."

"That was my music."

"Sure. That was *our* music. I never listen anymore."

Jake honed in on Carl's face, his sad eyes. The old face was there, more and more, but it had developed distinction during the past twenty years. He was the kind of guy who looked like a wimp in high school, Jake thought, but now at reunions he looked youthful and handsome while the others had gone to pot. For a moment Jake thought he saw Jenny's eyes in him.

Now, over the music, Carl, spreading mustard on his pastrami, said something something, Bob Dylan . . . and Jake said something something Herbert Marcuse, and Carl said, Cambodia incursion, March on Washington . . . Woodstock . . . Norman O. Brown. It was like a dance to the old words.

Eli looked over at Sebastian, who, not wanting to admit he didn't understand, wouldn't look his brother's way. But Sebastian drummed his fingers to the rhythm of the Grateful Dead.

Jake realized he himself wasn't speaking Brooklyn anymore and maybe Carl, too, wasn't speaking in the same way. And so deeper losses—or if not deeper, *communal*—entered the kitchen. It was as if the music of a shared history were vibrating like invisible guy wires supporting this platform in space and time and feeling, two men in a fluorescent-lit, rented kitchen.

"I helped manage the alternative news service," Carl said. You remember?"

"Freedom News."

"Freedom News. Right. I think—often I think—that was my best time," Carl said. "Those days, you worked with Jonas, right?"

"Jonas Segal."

"Jonas Segal. Brilliant, hyper kid who killed himself." Jake said this not to remind Carl but to memorialize. Everything came back: the old Volkswagen on the hill, vacuum cleaner pipe from the exhaust into the window. *I retrieved the paper from his pocket, where his will, his money, were to be found. The list of jobs that needed to be done at the farm.* Jonas died on a sunny day on a hilltop reading the *New York Times.*

"That was terrible," Carl said, "Maybe the beginning of the end."

Jake thought a minute. He got ice cream and handed the scoop to Sebastian. "So that's the thing in you, the thing Christine woke up again?"

"Something like that." The boys kept their eyes on their bowls. Jake realized once again what a loudmouth he was. He shut up; they sat, silent.

"We'll take our ice cream into the bedroom, okay?" Sebastian asked.

Sure. Jake was glad. "This once. Finish your packing and straightening up. Just be careful with the ice cream, okay?"

Sebastian rolled his eyes and looked glum.

Gently, Jake called him on the eye rolling. "Okay. What's that supposed to mean, Sebastian?"

"Why are you coming down so heavy?"

"What *heavy?* I just said, 'Be careful.' Is that so terrible?"

"Dad. In your house, we *can't* eat in the bedroom but we *can* eat in the living room. In Mom's, we can't eat in the living room but we can in the bedroom."

"I'll *talk* to her."

After they had gone upstairs, Jake sang to the Grateful Dead, "And if I knew the way, I would take you home." He shook his head and thought again about the commune. "Well, it was my time, too," he told Carl. "Narcissism and vanity. Masked by ideology," he added. "We were full of experiments. On ourselves, on our children. A professor I knew at U-Cal Santa Cruz, he believed in giving his three- and four-year-old kids acid on weekends. I often wonder what happened to those kids. . . . " But that wasn't what he really wanted to say. "I know about my *own* kid." *That* was it.

"You don't mean Sebastian and Eli. You mean your daughter."

"Christine must have told you? My daughter, my first marriage. Look at her now, Ellie's almost twenty-five, in and out of jobs, in and out of school, hospitals, relationships. Hah—relationships! . . . And drugs. Christine told you that, too?"

Carl nodded.

"When we divorced, her mother and me, twenty years ago, we were freeing ourselves from boxes. Same way you were talking. And what about our little kid? Well, of *course* a child would be happier after a separation, right?—because her mother and father would be truer to their *authentic selves.* . . . Makes me sick. Makes me sick to think."

"You think you wrecked your daughter?"

"See, the times—the times were full of chaos, I grant you. They still are. Worse, now, because it's without hope. But that's all the more reason I needed to watch over her. It was up to us to make up for what the community couldn't give."

"So do you see her? Your daughter?"

"In my mind's eye."

"I'm sorry," Carl said. They sat in silence. The music ended. They heard Eli and Sebastian clomp outside to throw a football around. Then Carl said, "Still, I believe in our old life, those days. The old hopes. I was this really straight kid. Maybe I wasn't free, but I believed in the possibility of becoming free. Like Jenny. The same. I still believe in *having believed,* caring enough to believe *some*thing. What can you give a child, Jake, if you don't bring that?"

"I see what you're saying," Jake admitted. "All right. I grant you. I grant you. Maybe something good got lost. Maybe it wasn't all vanity and narcissism. You know what I think?" Jake said. "We were *right* back then. We knew it wasn't just politics. It wasn't just *out there* we had to fight. *We had to turn ourselves inside out.* We just didn't know how fucking hard that would be. We're half crazy, cripples, all of us. Christine. You. Me, too, sure. Me, too."

"I would have been a good stepfather."

"You *would* have been. I sympathize. You wanted a ready-made family. Well, why not? You seem like a really good man. No—you *do*. You *do*." Jake waved a hand at the air, as if getting rid of a bug or a bad smell. Enough. He let his eyes close. He felt the afternoon growing sour. . . . *Christine:* I say her name, Jake thought, and all this freight attaches to my heart. *Enough.* He looked at the ceiling where the landlord still hadn't fixed the cracks, and he sank down deep inside himself and wished Carl would go home.

The boys came in, laughing at something, and Carl motioned toward them with his head and smiled. "Thanks for this afternoon," he said.

The kindness of the remark made Jake look at him and soften. Softening, he wondered how gentle a man had to be to get Christine's approval. "You know," Jake said, a hand on Carl's arm, "There's something I've been wanting to say. There's something about this talk between you and me makes it feel like an *absolute* moment. Like one of those times late at night, you're drunk or stoned—especially stoned, especially years ago, stoned—and get to talking about your lives. I remember back then talking like this with a friend all night long. You lift above the selves you pretend to be every day, and it's not that you won't be the same tomorrow, it's not that the talk changes any goddamn thing, but you feel like you've stepped outside your lives and you can look at them. I feel that with you." Not wanting to force Carl to confirm the feeling, he said, "I'm glad it worked out."

"Me, too." Carl got up, went into the living room. "Eli? Sebastian? I'm going now." He reached out his arms, and Eli ran into them while Sebastian hung back. But after Eli, Sebastian came up and hugged Carl.

"If either of you ever need me for anything . . . you under-stand?"

Jake put a hand on his arm and led him to the door. "Remember me to your sister. . . . Look—maybe—what d'you think?—maybe we can get together, play some tennis—you do play tennis, right? You look like a tennis player. I'll give you a call, okay?" They shook hands and Carl Degler walked down the front stoop and the boys waved and Jake felt he'd known him a million years and wondered, would they get to be friends—or maybe not see each other for another twenty years?

And he was thinking about this and about his date for tonight —her hair was also red, auburn—and puttering around the kitchen, when he heard a car door slam in the driveway and looked through the glass of the kitchen door to see Christine in her usual violet Lycra stretch pants and runner's sleeveless shirt coming along the flagstone to the back deck, and right away he knew she was pissed and knew why. He couldn't help particularly liking the way she walked when she was mad—long, strong hippy strides, blonde hair wild.

So the boys wouldn't see Christine, wouldn't have to hear the brawl he knew was coming, he went out onto the deck to meet her.

She waited till she was up the stairs, level with him—taller than Jake by an inch or two—and, arms akimbo, spoke huskily and precisely, as she always did when she wanted to make a really intense statement. "I am simply furious. I resent this terribly. God, I can't trust you for a minute. And you—you think it's funny? You're so smug!"

"What happened? You were driving by?"

"I wasn't snooping, if that's what you're implying. I was on my way home, I thought maybe the boys would be ready early. We're going to Connecticut, I wanted to get an early start."

"Sorry. Fuck you. You get them at five on the dot."

"I couldn't *believe* it, I saw his car, I couldn't believe it. What *right* do you have? To undercut me that way? How dare you let him near my children? Do you know what I've gone through?"

Leaning against the deck rail to suggest calm, Jake said, "He came by the game. I'm not saying the guy has rights, but he's got a lot of heart invested in those boys. I felt bad for him."

"YOU!" she said, as if the word were a curse. "You love this, don't you! You don't know the first thing about him. Heart! You don't know what he was like with me. Well, do you? You can't judge, Jake. One week Mr. Sweetness, next a cranky, depressed bastard. Do you know what he did after I told him to stay away? He sneaked into the house when the sitter was there. Only by pure chance, I came home and caught him."

"Maybe he wanted to say good-bye. And maybe he still wants you."

"He sneaked into *my house!* Frankly, I was scared. Wants me! How can I trust him after that? I had to get a restraining order."

"Ahh, he's no abuser, Christine. He's a kind man. He'd be good for you. In fact—maybe you should marry the guy."

"Don't you dare tell me who to marry! Don't you dare! I'd rather bring up the boys alone."

"Alone, huh?"

"Oh—I don't mean without your help. I mean I don't need to lock myself up inside some businessman's fantasy of a nineteenth-century marriage. *His* friends. *His* house. *His* career."

"Oh, come on, Christie. He's a decent guy, a sad guy."

"You're all just 'sad guys.' He just likes to come off like a sensitive man. Men, nowadays, they want the old prerogatives *plus* a stamp of the new sensitivity."

"Then why go out with men? If we're all such lowlifes."

"I didn't say *all.* And then—it gets hard, it gets lonely—*listen,* you've been sleeping with dozens of women for every man I've seen. I don't have a thing to explain to you."

"Dozens! Look, baby: the problem is, you're bringing up my sons. And they're going to be *men*."

"*Good* ones. Decent ones."

"Not like their father?"

"*That goes without saying*." But she said it—through half-clenched teeth.

"Me and Carl, we were discussing ideology," Jake said. "You, Christine, you use ideology to cover your anger. 'Men's selfishness, men's arrogance.'"

"And you *weren't* selfish? You *weren't* arrogant?"

"Maybe. Yeah, I'm a handful. But you—you wanted and wanted. You were hungry and nobody could feed you. You think I wanted to push you around? I wanted to live a decent life with you. I was twelve years older. I figured I knew what was up. 'Stick with me,' I said. 'Stick with me and maybe we can get through this life in one piece.'"

"You mean you wanted me to shut up and let you drive. That's ideology, too. The ideology of men in power keeping women in their place."

"Yeah, *you* lecture *me* on politics!"

"And that's another thing. You think you're so full of political virtue. The great healer. At $1,500 an article. It gets tiresome, sweetie, you can't imagine. But we were discussing you and Carl," Christine said. "You just make sure you never—"

"Hey, it's my house, my kids, sorry, baby."

"And you may not know it," she said, "but your swaggering 'MY' and that 'Baby'—that's ideology, too."

"I was saying to Carl, we're all cripples. We are," he sighed. "We are. Come *on*, Christie. Please. Carl was just saying good-bye. He'll leave the boys alone now. You ought to thank me. He said good-bye and finished something and you didn't have to be involved. See what I mean?"

She saw. She let out a huge breath and closed her eyes. Sitting on the edge of the old wooden table they'd once had in their basement playroom, she said quietly, "You make me so mad."

"Well, it must have been a shock. Like we were ganging up. He's still in love with you, you know."

"Stop that. Yes. Yes, I know."

For the first time in months, Jake felt a sexual warmth around Christine. Must be from the fighting, he thought. In his mind's eye he saw an image, quick, incomplete—must have been their bedroom, scene invented or remembered, books and clothes scattered in their joint mess, hot-water bottle from the time she wrenched her back in modern dance class. He saw a tennis racket, a crumpled leotard, a pyramid of paperbacks with half-glasses on the top. The debris of married life. The weary debates halfway to morning, nobody giving an inch. Or sometimes the surprise of laughter and surrender, your own or hers, and lovemaking that seemed like the satisfying last piece of a puzzle.

"You got to be an angel," Jake said. "A complete angel. I mean, to be married. Especially in our times."

"Sometimes," she said, quietly, so quietly he almost missed it, "we *were*."

Now that they were quiet, Sebastian and Eli came out onto the deck, and Jake realized that they must have heard the rumble of a fight and waited. It was sad—how politically adroit children had to become after a divorce.

"Hi, guys," Christine said breezily. She opened her arms.

Jake said, "Sebastian, Eli, please get your things ready. Your mom's going to take you a little early. You're going off to Connecticut, remember?"

Christine looked at him in surprise. "Thank you."

But suddenly, the children stopped being all that politic. Sebastian hunkered down over folded arms as if battered by a cold wind. "You see what I mean? You see? The way you jerk us around?"

"Come on now," Jake said. "A couple of hours, what's the big deal?"

"It *is* a big deal. And I can tell you why."

Sebastian waited for the go-ahead, and Jake found himself irritated but at the same time goddamned pleased, proud, that Sebastian was bucking them like this. "Okay. Why?"

"You don't even ask us anything. You just push us and pull us and we're supposed to do—whatever whatever whatever!"

"I'm sorry, I'm sorry, I'm sorry," Christine said. She heaved one of her dramatic great breaths. "But I am really ex*haus*ted," she said, her voice rising in pitch with each word. As if somehow this formulation did something good for her, she said it again, "I am really exhausted. I try to make a pleasant weekend for us, and you know all the work I've got!—and I don't need all this . . . "

. . . *crap,* Jake finished in his head. "Boys," he said calmly, hands upraised like a Pentecostal preacher offering blessing, "boys, please, help your mother out."

Christine shut her eyes and, her fingers fluttering like a drowning swimmer stretching for a hand, she waved at the boys to *come, just* come, *for godsakes,* and now Eli—this amazed Jake—got into the act, and he yelled "No way!" and for support hugged his brother around the waist, and there stood Jake and Christine on the deck facing off against Eli and Sebastian, and now Jake began to laugh at the stalemate, he couldn't help it, and Christine said, "I don't see anything so funny," but soon she was giggling and Jake crumpled in laughter on the deck, legs crossed yogi-style, and maybe the laughter was half fake, pumped up to help smooth things over, but it was half real, too.

Then Sebastian was smiling and shrugging, and Jake went up to him and kissed him hard on both cheeks, and he turned and went inside for the bags. Christine was hugging Eli.

And soon she and the boys were gone, hugs and good-bye and gone, waving, into her Volvo station wagon and back down the driveway. Jake felt his laughter dry up, like nothing would ever be funny again, like his mouth, his heart, were full of sand. He straightened up the boys' rooms, and lying back on his battered two-marriage sofa, called his current woman friend to see if she maybe wanted to get together a little early.

# The Man Who Could See Radiance

*Before* he saw radiance, he saw the way we all see. He
saw his wife, Rachel, as threatening or contributing
to his equilibrium; an irritation or, sometimes,
someone he loved so that touching her was like touching the
source of all metaphor, making his mind gasp and his mouth
open. It's not something he ever put into words, what that was all
about. Usually, she was someone to eat dinner with, someone to
tell stories—he met lots of people, he told her stories. And all
other women he saw as, first of all, more beautiful or less beautiful than Rachel, older, younger, could-be wives or lovers or
godforbid-to-be-married-to-that-one. Or he saw them as Rachel's friends, taking her away from his life or maybe giving them
someplace to go on a Saturday night. Then there were the old, he
felt sorry for, and the young, he felt tenderness for, the young who
made him remember the failures of his life.

Of course, his own children were different, they still made
him glow, eyes fill so he had to turn his head away. Out of the

house now, Jennifer in law school, Noah in his senior year at college, and he worried when they flew home, worried when they went off on ski weekends.

At work he saw guys he liked or didn't like, men and women the same, good to work with or hard to do business with, dumb son of a bitch. McAndrews knew how to smooth over tensions at a meeting; Myers stepped on his lines.

And he saw time as his enemy, keeping him from ever getting everything done, and energy he saw as something he held in a psychic bank and had to replenish if he spent, and never could he keep the account fat for very long.

So he saw and saw and went through Boston seeing, and that's the way it was. He saw the world fabricated from his needs, the world pleasant or unpleasant, curious or dull, never beyond his fabrication, though he didn't see the fabrication.

Peter Weintraub was past midlife, no crisis in sight; all the crises he could handle, he'd handled—doubt about his work, a beautiful woman who came along at the right time, and then Rachel, too, turned out to be having an affair with the headmaster at the prep school where she taught history. A hard couple of years, but somehow they lasted and knew each other now, they said that in bed sometimes when they were about to make love, we know each other now. Fondness of the extra flesh at hip or belly, as if to touch that flesh were also to know, with compassion, *limits*, this is it, my particular life, and it isn't bad or dull.

This should be the end of a story; trailing into flashes of erotic glory, or a moment awash with tenderness, or joy of the capture of new markets for the software his company sold, vacation trips (Florence, Aruba), losses, sorrows, death, please God the lives of children continuing, history complicating or exploding everything, maybe the planet. Otherwise, Friday evening concerts in Symphony Hall.

But one day at the end of grimy winter, riding the MTA from Newton into downtown Boston, he looked into the eyes—maybe

they were temporarily unprotected, they must have been unprotected—of another middle-aged man (laptop computer, London Fog raincoat) sitting across the aisle. The trolley went under-
ground at Church Street, and as Weintraub glanced up, the legs
and book bags in the aisle shifted, and he felt this man's eyes, felt,
oh, my God, the *damage* and, instantly, saw the minor panic of
this man putting up eyes in front of eyes like an alien discovering
his humanoid mask wasn't right. Yet Peter felt it *more* now, the
damage, heard this man not-saying *I'm afraid of your eyes seeing
me, making me pull too hard at the guy wires that keep me from
breaking apart in this terrible wind*. Trolley shivering and howling
in the tunnel. Then overcoats and briefcases between them.
When Peter was able to see again, the man was gone.

Weintraub shuddered, and, his own eyes closed, he saw again
the panic in the gone eyes and, under the eyes, the pain. Maybe
the poor son of a bitch was cracking up. Just, aaach, just some
poor son of a bitch. But he couldn't account for his own turbu-
lence, as if a door had just opened into hell. And here was the
worst of it: he suspected that he'd seen this way before. Not once.
*Always*. He'd kept himself from knowing. But he'd never *not* seen
this way.

At work, he forgot. March 1: he had a report to get out for a
meeting with management, and he played with the stats and
graphics, altering the units of measurement so a fairly flat curve
looked pregnant. The report went to the laser printer, and Jean
Collis had eight bound copies on his desk ten minutes before the
meeting, and he smiled up at her—and with a terrible rush felt
*her life, her life,* and had to close his eyes to keep the knowledge
off. Pain again, though not the same as on the trolley; then was it
his own pain he was seeing? But no, he was sure it belonged to Ms.
Collis, brittle Ms. Collis who had a well-publicized secret life he'd
always known, you could see the posters over her desk, soft-focus
landscapes with New Age aphorisms about the soul, but what he
saw now was a life intended to stay secret, even from herself, and

it was so open to him, the balance sheet of humiliations she kept, he couldn't breathe. He pushed back from his desk, hand over his heart. "Thank you so much. Thank you, such a good job, thank you."

"We forgot to single-space the indents."

"But it's beautiful."

Weintraub stumbled through the meeting. He was afraid to look anyone in the face; he was afraid to breathe too deeply, as if it were *breath* that were taking in the pain, like the summer in college when he worked in a state hospital and there were certain wards where it was best to take a deep breath and hold it until you walked out.

He tried to explain to Rachel.

"Well, as for Ms. Collis, what do you expect?" she said. "Your Ms. Collis is a sour bitch. I can't stand Jean Collis." She poured their wine. "Don't get me started."

Now he was afraid to look into Rachel's eyes, but it didn't matter, he was *anyway* flooded by her life, nothing she *said*, her life naming itself secretly in her voice so that he found hot tears coming as he tried to answer, thinking *I didn't know, I didn't know*—knowing it had nothing to do with Jean Collis, whom she'd met maybe twice. What then? He couldn't say, but he held her hand against his chest and stroked, mothering them both.

I'm just having problems about boundaries, he thought, thought over and over; fusing, confusing. This has to stop.

Then a week without trouble except at night, dreams of hard travel through a half-strange city, the bus not coming, subway station the other side of an impossible highway, maps he couldn't read without glasses, and along the way irritating helpers who put him on the wrong elevator, tumbling him into the morning radio news, cranky and fatigued. Then the next night, the same confusing city and so much to carry, clumsy not heavy, and the overcoat he had to go back for probably lost.

I need a spring vacation, he said to Rachel. You and me both, she said.

The first seeing came almost as relief, like rain pouring down to break a heat wave and finally you could breathe, worth it even if you'd left the cushions out on the deck chairs. This time, it was a friend. Aaron and Beth Michaels came for dinner, and Weintraub had nothing to say and longed for them to be gone, longed for sleep, held a glass of good wine that tasted sour.

He felt hot, itching—soon he'd learn to recognize that itching in his chest—he looked up to see Beth, who'd been talking about their daughter's suffering in marriage, to see Beth's own suffering, her life suddenly visible. He half stood to reach out to her and fold his arms around her, but that wasn't possible. But he wanted to, and it was his having to sit there and listen quietly to Beth's story that sent him over into seeing the radiance that first time.

It shone from her eyes, something to do with her eyes, but it was centered at her chest, pulsing out like the northern lights he once saw, visible, not visible, a trick of the light?—oh, no, she glowed—out of the suffering something radiated. *I can turn this off*, he thought. *I can examine it critically and get rid of this golden light.*

But he'd always liked her, and all at once he was breathing so fully again after suffocating weeks that he didn't have the heart to try. *I know you, know you.* He drank his wine and felt vaguely adulterous—and hoped they couldn't see. He changed from Handel to Brahms, a trio, and checked the casserole. When he came back to the couch, he was afraid it wouldn't be there, but it was. Everything else went on according to the rules of the dance.

The Brahms that everyone else seemed to tune out was almost too much for him to bear, with this light pulsing around Beth in the wing-backed armchair. A trick of sight, a trick of hearing as well, for the cello pulsed within his body. A trick of the heart. *I wish I could talk about this to Rachel.* But he was afraid it might never come back. And then . . . she'd think things.

"Anybody for more wine?"

Maybe if he saw truly, Weintraub thought, this is how he'd see everyone. Every human creature in the radiance that made him tremble, made him—terrible dinner companion—gawk at Beth all evening. And Rachel *did* think things. Getting ready for bed, she wouldn't talk. "Rachel?" he said. "Please?"

"You were staring at that woman all night. I wouldn't care, but it was humiliating. Everyone must have noticed."

He couldn't see the light pulsing from Rachel. He even dimmed the bedroom hoping to see. I mean, imagine—to live in the presence of that radiance!

She turned the lights up again. "You're *not* all of a sudden getting romantic with me—not after staring at someone else all night?"

"*No.* Listen, Rachel, it's just that I *noticed* something about her. Like her *soul* for godsakes."

"What a peculiar animal I married." Rachel started giggling the way she used to years and years ago, until the giggles emptied out, then brimmed up in her again and bubbled over so that she had to lean against the bed and dry her eyes. "Her soul! Tell me another. Oh, you dumb bird!" Stepping out of her skirt, she went to the closet for her shorty nightgown. "Peter? I think I'm changing my mind about romance. You can make love to my soul."

About Beth, at least he could understand. Wasn't it true he'd always imagined taking her to bed? Her soul? Rachel was right to laugh. But what about Jack Myers, Vice-President of Sales and Being a Prick? They couldn't be in the same meeting without putting each other down. Just the hint that one of them supported a plan was enough to get the other suspicious. Myers! The guy had a big mouth for (1) swallowing the world, and (2) emitting hot air. But the next Monday morning at the weekly marketing meeting, Peter Weintraub looked up and there was the narcissistic son of a bitch glowing, pulsing. He could hardly bear to see, it was so rich, the light. The son of a bitch, so *precious*—why was he so precious?

Myers laid out a campaign for sales to catalogue companies. Weintraub had a hard time listening. So precious! He got up and sat next to Myers—"Mind if I look over your shoulder?"

Myers kept talking. Weintraub conducted an experiment; casually straightening papers, he let his fingers get close to Myers's chest: *What did the light feel like?*

Myers gave him a look.

"Mmm, nice plan," Weintraub said.

Now McAndrews, the guy who made everything move in the company, McAndrews also gave him a look, and Ferris, the aging golden boy who'd developed the original software concepts, said, "Well! It must be one *hell* of a plan." And Weintraub, thinking fast, said, "Myers, you're finally coming around to what I said a year ago."

Now, for the time being, it was okay. Everyone laughed except Myers.

He could feel the light or feel something at the borders of his own body, not see, but feel in fingers and cheeks and chest a humming like when he stood at night outside a Con Edison plant—a kid, summertime, doors open and the turbines humming like a giant chorus in all registers, and it seemed they were producing the energy that made the earth turn and the trees grow. Whose energy was this? Myers's? His own? No saying.

At work, colleagues had always seen Weintraub as a little peculiar, but—he knew—they were fond of his strangeness. So there were times you could walk into his office and find him checking proofs on a catalogue, headphones on, arms conducting a silent Mahler. He knew they accepted that. It made them feel that the workplace wasn't a concentration camp. They *used* his freedom as symbols of their own. But now they began looking at him after he passed down the hall; he caught reflections in glass doors. People spoke to him carefully and slowly. Sometimes that was when he was staring into their radiance, sometimes not. And then Rachel sat him down one day and said, "Peter? Peter, I got a call from Joe Ferris. He wonders . . . "

"I'm *not* going to do therapy. Isn't that what you're asking?"

"Do you want to go off somewhere? You said . . . "

"Actually," he said, "*I don't want to lose this.*"

"Lose what?"

He was afraid to kill it by saying. "It's too good to talk about."

It was so good that he had to wonder. Look. He was no saint. *Especially* now. Sometimes five minutes after he saw radiance, he felt rage. And it was worse when he tried to live an ordinary life. One night, he had a fight with the young jerk behind the checkout at the video store. The kid mixed him up with someone who'd tossed late tapes on the counter. He called out to Weintraub, "Hey! You owe $6.50 on these."

"Me? Those? No—they're not my tapes."

"Hey! Don't bullshit me."

"You got the wrong guy."

"Hey! You can just stop looking—you're not taking out any more tapes until you pay."

"And I told you, you moron, they're not mine."

"Yeah? Let's see your card, then. Hey!"

"YOU! YOU!—shut the hell up! Close that mouth, you understand?" And Weintraub discovered he was suddenly raging, shouting, and the other browsers were staring. "I said they're not mine, prick! You'll see my card when I'm goddamn ready. Now—not another word out of you! Not another word!"

"Hey! I said show me your card if it's not you." Now the kid wasn't sure. "Who are you then?"

Weintraub, affronted, righteous, trembling, hot, hot in the

face, took his time, picked out a movie and slapped the cover on the counter—along with his membership card.

"Yeah, well, okay—you could've showed me this and saved the hassle."

There were twenty, thirty tapes piled up on the counter. Weintraub swept them off with the sickle of his arm, and they scattered against the metal shelves, and Weintraub stomped out, neck tight, victorious—victorious over a child. All that rage! The kid had him by twenty pounds and twenty years but wouldn't have stood a chance (Weintraub was sure) against his battle fury. He could imagine a bloody fistfight in the video store, all the Newton lawyers and doctors waiting for their professional services to be required.

*And that he should be the one to see radiance!* It made him squirm. Maybe I *do* need therapy. He drove around awhile. Then, sitting in the silence of his garage with the engine off, he wondered if it wasn't wishful seeing, pretending the world secretly expressed *love*. When it didn't.

Calmed, he could still feel his own blood, and, at the borders between his body and the world, the humming that was always with him now. Peter had never been a fighter, hadn't fought since grade school. *I wanted to kill that boy.* He tilted the rearview mirror to look at himself, expecting to see a terrible radiance, green or red ugly light pulsing around his head. But all he saw was his ordinary face; the eyes, at being questioned, questioning.

"I'm home!" he sang out, entering.

"I'm in the family room. Come have a drink."

From her voice he knew she knew.

She poured him a sherry and sat beside him, capturing his hand. "The store called. The owner: he was very, very upset."

"*I* was very upset."

"Not the young man. The *owner*. He's cancelled your membership. He says, if we make trouble, he'll sue."

"I couldn't care less."

"And . . . Nancy Pollock called."

"Christ—was *she* there? Well, to hell with the Pollocks."

"No—Nancy was being kind, she was terribly worried. I said you'd been under some strain." She stroked his hand. "Poor Peter."

*Now* came the strain: he worked hard to do the work of the world. He tried to avoid being peculiar, even in the old ways. Good-bye to his Walkman and headphones and waving his arms to *Lied von der Erde*. He never loosened his tie. It would take time, he knew, to regain his position of normality in his company, but soon, at least sooner than he'd expected, they had stopped talking slowly and carefully to him. Ferris brushed invisible dust off Weintraub's Italian suit and congratulated him on a report—on reentering the world. Weintraub knew he was really staying outside, outside other people's hearts and safe from radiance and rage. He could tame the eyes of colleagues if he looked *at,* not *into* them. Sometimes he wondered whether they knew what he knew and had taught themselves to see only just enough to get by on—then to forget they'd done it.

No radiance, but the cost: the world stopped glowing, and then stopped mattering. It was *only* matter. He imagined it was like being an alcoholic or, say, a heroin addict, who'd felt the rich fabric of life through his drug and then, his blood neutralized, felt nothing.

But then, he began to be aware, dimly, unsure, out of the corner of his eye, but soon intensely—of a visible dissonance; shock waves. Always.

He saw them first faintly in the street on his way to work. Twice, he saw them in the supermarket, but they were just jangling, just irritating, they weren't terrible—not until the regular Monday morning meeting.

The meeting hadn't got started; people wandered in, coffee

mugs full, talked football scores. Laughter. Of *course* it was a little phony, a pretense at relaxed congeniality, but so what? That, Peter knew, was how business got accomplished—people put on underwear and shoes and combed their hair and made up their faces and worried about their own projects, their own places in the company, about their children, about their health, and wasn't there something noble about the false good humor that gave them, temporarily, a common speech, a key in which to sing all their different notes? And then work got done.

But this Monday morning he saw not radiance but only forms of brittle energy surrounding, bounding everyone, like the concentric circles around a rock dropped in a pool, fending off the circles around other rocks. But *these* shock waves weren't concentric; they were crazy-irregular. No angel would wear such a thing as nimbus. Ugly, jagged, the waves of air jarred against each other, distorting, and Peter sank back in his conference chair to keep out of the way.

The squawk! As if every man and woman was a miniature broadcasting tower sending out these waves, jamming each other's broadcasts. Worse: the lines of force—though nothing, though air or a trick of seeing—had nasty, sharp, staccato edges—watch out!—like concertina wire strung up to keep off thieves. Peter dug in as if his chair were a trench. It was war. He gaped.

Then the meeting settled down, and he saw these protective waves settle back close to their owners, condense, intensify. Then Ferris's voice, getting things under way, warm and cheerful: all the barbed lines of force opened slightly like lips to let his voice enter, but the force felt it as invasion. He could see how his colleagues handled the alien force that they had to let in: prepared, they shaped it, surrounded it, until it became part of their own force. But when he looked at the room, he understood why Ferris was so successful with personnel. Gradually, the lines of force grew less staccato, smoother, and the edges less fierce. It was like wild beasts under the sway of a tamer. Oh, but he knew how temporary. No hope! No hope! No hope!

Less afraid, now that the individual boundaries had grown less jagged, he had time to mourn. Behind his hand, he wept for all of them. This wasn't smart! Thank God he had a tissue in his pocket, he could blow his nose—a spring cold—but what did it matter, the hopelessness was so much more terrible than his individual embarrassment. So, his weeping unprotected by tissue, he collected his papers and went back to his office.

"Jean, I'm not feeling well. I don't think . . . I think I'm—"

But the barbed lines of air around Ms. Collis were fierce, and he rushed past her, down the elevator and into a gray spring day, downtown Boston—but it was like entering Beirut in civil war or the hell where city gang fighters go when they die. Burrowing down inside himself, he walked fast toward the subway at Government Center, then broke into a run, but there was nowhere to run, all around him on the open plaza in front of City Hall were indifferent people with fields of force that weren't indifferent at all. So many people—each surrounded by a jagged perimeter of defense, and the lines jarring silently against each other, a giant interwoven beast or bitter maze that shifted to let him through. He himself was without protection. Worst, he was without protection from his vision. So this was it!

He flagged a taxi just empty and ran to its open door.

For the first three days Peter lay on the beach and didn't look at people, kept his eyes to himself like a shy child. He let Rachel decide where they would eat, when they would sleep. Did he really sleep? He couldn't tell. Ashamed, he clung, big man, wrestler in college, close to her warmth against the crisp white hotel sheets, and, tense until her breathing deepened, then he sank into a flowing dark inside the dark; it was like, by day, letting the Caribbean mild tides carry him as he floated, breathing through the snorkeling tube and letting his eyes fill with gentle, glowing fish, the colors leading him down under giant coral and through the reef passage, where he would breathe deep and plunge, a sudden drop of fifteen feet, into darker water of the bigger fish until he couldn't take the pressure. Then he'd surface, clear the tube, and drift back through the passage.

He couldn't read. What did he do? He lay on the beach.

"You're healing, don't worry," Rachel said.

On the third night, they made love again, and it was gentle as the fish. For three days, he hadn't looked at her, not looked all the way down, but while he was inside her he opened his eyes and her eyes were open, and moving slowly inside her he saw at the perimeter of his seeing a dim glowing that might have been him or might have been her or both, like a pattern impressed into the dark, angel-in-the-snow they made an angel in darkness. The radiance had come back to him. He was afraid to ask, *Do you see it?* He closed his eyes; coming, he drifted into the radiance.

It was after two when he awoke and went to the balcony to look at the ocean. No moon. He felt his blood rising into his fingers and put up his humming palms as if they pressed against a window of darkness, and for the first time he could see his own radiance, faint, glowing. *I'm all this,* he said to himself. *This is who I am! This is who I am!* Turning, he saw Rachel with her hair spread out on the pillow, and it seemed to him that faintly, from the dark of her hair, a light hovered around her. And in that light he could read her sorrows—miscarriages and work she'd grown tired of, failure as a musician and compromises in loving him and fear that Jennifer didn't love her. Saw. As he looked, her radiance flamed.

*I can never be the same, never. . . .* he whispered and whispered again, longing for it to be true.

They held hands on the flight home. He could look again, though it frightened him to see the jagged perimeters of strangers, but his vision protected him, his *knowing*. He walked safe inside his own space of knowing.

At Aaron and Beth's house he took a chance on coming back into his old world.

Candles on the coffee table, old friends as in a beer commercial. Beth and Aaron laid out a platter of artichoke hearts and calamata olives, scallions and red peppers—an antipasto. The shocks of air, the brittle, jagged energy protected Aaron. Protected from what? *From me? What am I doing?* He smiled across at Aaron as if to say, *Hey, no need, no need—it's all right*. But though Aaron smiled, humoring, Aaron's fierce shock of air intensified. Peter wondered, *Can I feed him from my own radiance?* That was the moment, lifting his hands as if to pass on a blessing, he saw for the first time his *own* barbed field of force: it grew out from his hands and through his jacket and surrounded him, and as he grew afraid it grew uglier until it seemed to wrap around him like a stockade. And murderous—it wanted death for Aaron, wanted absolute exclusion of other life. "Oh, please . . . I want to get out," he said, in a small voice, meaning this prison of his own making. "It's not like I thought. Nothing's like I thought."

"Rachel—you want me to get your coats?" Beth said, and her voice implied long conversations about him on the phone.

"No—that's not it—" Peter started to explain, then stopped, because in this moment of emergency everyone had come temporarily together—maybe it was that, and that his own need was so great to get past himself, and he *saw* as if all the cells or atoms of each of them were pointillistically vibrating in golden space and each desperately holding separate being together, but he could see that boundaries were almost arbitrary. And all the defensive fields, too, were not separate but intermeshed. Aaron's field depended on his and his on Aaron's. If he looked too long, all the boundaries, the visible forms, would disappear. Like a computer engineer getting underneath the software, underneath the hidden codes, underneath the program and even the machine language to the essential on-and-offs that you couldn't see. And he tried to explain, and Beth said, "Can I get you a scotch, Peter?" and he knew it wasn't possible and bent his head and stayed silent and made his heart stay silent. "Pass the wine," he'd say. "Pass the steak. How's work, Aaron?" They were all relieved.

He stayed mostly silent all the next day, a Sunday, and Rachel let him be. He listened to music. When he heard her getting dinner started, he came down and helped her cut up vegetables, because *that's what you do,* you cut up vegetables and sauté them in oil and add cumin and coriander. You say to your wife, "I'm feeling okay," and take her kiss and say, "You get your lesson plans finished?"

And slowly, because it was necessary, the vision faded. He wept at odd times and for no reason. The vision came to him less and less the next few months, finally not at all. And sometimes he thought, *It was just chemistry.* And sometimes he thought, *I know what's under there.* He took up his work again and was careful what he said. So after a while he was able to wave his arms while listening over the headphones to Mahler, and the others shook their heads and grinned, relieved: Weintraub was back. And he was able to fight with Jack Myers, and when he talked with Joe Ferris, didn't see more than Ferris wanted him to see, didn't see with his heart. He saved his heart in a safe deposit vault and brought out small sums when he could, especially for Rachel, for Rachel and for their children.

# Old Friends

*e* couldn't put you up in your usual rooms," Wink says. "Actually, I'm camping out there myself while Nan gets better. But we'll try to make you comfortable. . . . You'll recognize the furniture," he adds, smiling under his bushy eyebrows that have turned gray and wild.

Pete erases the air with his open hands. "Christ, Wink, I'm here to help you guys out, you and Nan. That's what I'm here for."

"Well, you must know what a relief it is for me." Wink shrugs his big shoulders, and Pete loves him for his gentle humility; Wink seems to him a man who seldom needs you to notice his strength.

Now Pete is left alone in the guest room with furniture left over from earlier, simpler times of their lives. Pete remembers the Victorian dresser from a flat in Pimlico in the midfifties—the first time Wink and Nan had money to go down to Portobello Road and find pieces they liked. *I helped them lug it home,* Pete thinks. And that tapestried wing-backed chair. *We carried it*

*through the street and took turns sitting on it as if a London side-*
*walk were our parlor.*

Not jet lag but just being in his friends' house has wiped him
out. Funny. He's past the shock of it. But it's still something he
can't take in. He keeps saying to himself, *Anyone can have a stroke.*
Then—*But Nan!*

For weeks, Pete listened to his friend weeping in the middle
of transatlantic silence. A guttural, baritone weeping, it shocked
him. Pete remembered when they first knew one another, when
they were poor and calls were so expensive, when they respected a
transatlantic call like a telegram. The hiss of long-distance silence
would have scared them. Now, not. "Oh, Wink, ah Jesus Christ,
man," he'd say, and then silence, silence, and Wink blowing his
nose. And then, gradually, over the weeks, Wink began telling
him that, thank God, *something* was left, some fragments of
memory, he meant—Nan was beginning to remember things.
"Well, thank God, Wink."

Pete said to Betsy, "I should fly over and see Wink."

"Of course you should."

Every day he said, "I should go over."

"But why *don't* you go?" Betsy said. "You'd be such a help to
Wink. I can't, you know I can't—Jennifer will be having the baby
any day now. But *you* can."

"Oh, Betsy, it feels so sad. I keep seeing the four of us swimming from that motorboat off the coast of Malta. Remember? We
have a snapshot somewhere?—Wink mugging a dive? We were all
so beautiful."

"Well, it *is* sad. Naturally," said Betsy, noticing spots on the
mirror; she found Windex in the bathroom and went to work.

"I'll tell you how it feels," he said, sitting on the bed. "Not like
dying. That's not what I'm afraid of. It's entering the time when
things start to happen that can't be fixed. When the specialists
take charge—that's what scares me. And then . . . "

"And then?"

"Well, and then—and then, it's the end of something we were."

Betsy just looked hard at him, as if measuring the strength of a companion on a hard climb. Always the firm one, she didn't have to say a thing.

"All *right*," he said. "All right, all right."

"Oh, Pete. What are you so afraid of?"

"I *said* 'all right.' "

He left a message on Wink's answering machine and took an evening flight to Heathrow. It was late March, a month since Nan's stroke.

Miles's *Kind of Blue* plays muted in the muted sitting room. Playing this, Pete thinks, is meant to be understood as a quote, as Wink's homage to their past. Wink sits listening, big hands hung between his thighs. Pete watches him: big galoomph of a face, craggy monument of a face, above the heavy, slumped shoulders. Nan sleeps upstairs in their Georgian terraced house that fronts on a little gated park. They're alone in the house, the three of them, as they were alone so often in the fifties, before Betsy made them a foursome. The cleaning lady has gone home, the community nurse has stopped by to check on Nan, the physiotherapist to help her begin the long climb back. But Wink has been her real nurse. Their daughter, Alice, flew out from California, but she could stay only a week; she has her family to take care of. God knows Wink could have hired a full-time nurse, but this—nursing Nan—is what he wanted. He's dropped everything else—the banking, even the steering of his own portfolio. Everything.

Waking, Nan buzzes, and the buzzer rouses Wink; he calls up, "Coming, I'm coming." It's so odd to see Wink with his great head and groomed, somewhat manelike graying hair, an important man, Wink, in an apron, fixing tea—herbal tea—and carrying it up to her, the pot and cup and miniature spoon and folded linen napkin so small on the large, filigreed silver tray.

Walking up behind his big friend, Pete notices how Wink has spread out some in the beam, and somehow this makes him feel an intense, bizarre affection for him.

Nan looks small in the great four-poster. *Does she know me? Does she even know Wink?* Wink puffs up her pillows, white pillows, white coverlet, and the two big men sit at the side of her bed. Wink says, "Nan, it's Pete. It's Pete Hayes, Pete and Betsy, it's Pete." Nan tries to articulate speech. The words come out as if she were a new speaker of English who didn't quite get the rules of syntax. She's able to smile on one side and say, throaty and thick, "Pete . . . Pete it *is.*"

"You look fine," Pete says. It's a lie but not a lie. Her mouth twists down at one corner. Her hair seems to have whitened even since last summer, when they all met at the Montreux jazz festival. She looks ashen, dim. Still, it's good to see her. Five minutes by her bedside and she's just Nan again. Maybe floating on whatever drugs, maybe it is that—but she seems younger somehow, the architecture of defenses gone from her face; a girl with white hair.

Nan has always been the poet among them, the one to collect wildflowers and grasses for table bouquets. She wears Russian capes and loose, flowing silk dresses, collects antique rings and often wears one on every finger. She depends on Betsy for recipes; throwing an important party, Nan would call Betsy, London to Connecticut, to ask whom she should place next to whom. Always, Nan has flung herself on the sweetness of the world, and until now, the world has held her gently.

Clear-eyed Betsy skis with precision and control; even after all these years, every November she still trains on Nautilus machines and takes master classes when she starts a ski week. Nan is a graceful, spontaneous skier. She makes it look as if all you have to do is fall, and as if falling is splendid. Skiing behind her, Betsy, Wink, Pete used to laugh at the way she'd lift her poles outspread like wings and sing, sing opera, conducting with her wings as she floated down. Once, not seeing a patch of ice, she tumbled hard into a tree, and then refused to wait for the ski patrol. Wink splinted her leg with broken poles and scarves, and Pete on one side, Wink on the other, they skied her down the mountain, Nan crying and shaking and laughing at herself.

Now she shakes her head and smiles as if apologizing for her stupid speech, or as if, *not* apologizing, she were making fun of herself as she often did, the impractical one—just look what I've done *now*.

"She's doing so much better, my girl," Wink says. "Sometimes she says 'glass' when she means 'book,' or she can't think how to begin a sentence, but then once she gets cranking, it comes, it comes. And you *are* remembering things, aren't you?"

"My mother, voice, sing she did . . . me." Nan smiles. A triumph. The two men lean forward, as if the leaning might make it easier for her, for Nan's voice is soft and slurred and takes a long time. And now they sit back, Peter fatigued from the flight and the sadness, from having to smile at Nan.

"Beginning to remember. Like finding a piece here and a piece there in a jigsaw puzzle. The more she finds, the more she's got to attach new pieces to. Little victories, isn't that right, my girl?"

Nan nods. Her eyes are a little vague, but then, they've always been a little vague. It's part of her charm. Pete takes her hand. "It's so good to see you, lady."

"Tea?" Nan says and points with her eyes.

Wink understands. "We're all right. Had ours. This tea's for you."

She hoists herself up and sips, one hand holding the other holding the cup.

"She's begun therapy, did I tell you? Every morning, exercises. Next week we go to hospital, to the fancy machines."

Nan throws her eyes up to the heavens. Pete and Wink laugh, and Wink says, "Plenty of excitement, love. Now you rest awhile."

"It's looking good," Wink says on the way downstairs. "She won't be fully paralyzed on the bad side, and I think she'll remember more, get more language back. But it could happen again, Pete."

"There's the drugs to keep down her blood pressure."

"Sure. Still . . ."

Now it's evening. They've foraged for dinner. Pete remembers the whiskey, not what they ate. Wink said, "There are all these spice bottles with no labels. Nan just *knew*, you see. I could ask her what's what, but you think I'm going to learn to cook?"

"You'll need a housekeeper."

"I know. I'll have to get a housekeeper. But that makes it feel so final, Pete."

"You think it *is* final?"

Wink strokes the leather of his armchair as if it were a cat. "Well. That part. The cooking. Her right hand barely functions."

"The skiing."

"The skiing. The skiing. Can I get you another drink?"

"You drink," Pete says. "Go ahead and tie one on. Like we used to. I'll stand watch. I'll be designated nurse."

"She'll need her pills at midnight."

"All right."

"The two containers nearest to the bed. Not the others. . . . But I'll probably be fine. All right. Let's drink to what we were," Wink says, and laughs at himself and pours himself a large scotch, a short one for Pete. "Well—not maybe all that grand."

"Sure we were grand."

"Well, we thought so, and maybe that's all it takes," Wink says. He raises his glass and drinks a ritual drink, then leans back in the big leather chair. "We fooled the bastards, didn't we?"

Pete understands and grins as he's meant to grin. He looks around this lovely, elegant room—old ship's clock in well-oiled cherry, the small John Singer Sargent watercolor, an inlaid eighteenth-century table. Behind built-in walnut cabinetry, the stereo system playing Coltrane must have cost thousands of pounds. All to be taken with irony. *We fooled the bastards.* As if all this didn't *define* the four of them.

There had always been this con. Winthrop Thompson—Wink—had risen to be head of the London branch of an American bank. His wife, Nan, contributed her services as a member of the board of directors of Oxfam. But through all these years Wink claimed to feel like a spy, a successful fraud, secret fifties hipster in Bond Street suits. What they loved, Wink and Nan, was to wear the trappings of success (they were on one of the lists at Buckingham Palace) with that special grace cast by irony.

It was a shared comic irony—shared since the time of HUAC and the loyalty oaths. If, all these years, Pete and Betsy Hayes, Wink and Nan Thompson, would meet in Interlaken for skiing or share a villa on Ibiza or in Provence, always they did it with irony. It was partly their love for the outdoors that let them feel superior to the business people they worked with. They hiked in the Alps, once in the Himalayas—it was a sign of their personal anarchism. It was as if most of the year they were in costume, the four of them, and since it was the costume everyone else wore as *clothing*, only they knew it. It was their secret, never even spoken among themselves, but somehow sustaining them, helping, certainly, to sustain their friendship for over four decades.

Now he wants to tell Wink, *All we've fooled is ourselves. The operative irony actually belongs to our class and our culture. And they are laughing at us: "You think you can escape being defined by class? Escape through style? Through hipness? Through sexual élan? Through political cynicism? That's our little joke. You belong to us."*

But of course he doesn't say this. "We've had a hell of a good run for it," he says.

"Nobody's been young like us," Wink says.

"Sure. Nobody."

"I'm glad you're here, Pete. I feel I can let go and bullshit a little. Who can I talk to this way? You, hell, you probably know me better than anyone does."

"Except Nan."

"Sure, oh, sure . . ."

Pete understands: Wink isn't sure *what* Nan knows. Pete says, "I *should* know you. You saved my life. You held me with your hands—" and he mimes Wink holding the rope when the piton gave way.

"God made me a fullback," Wink laughs.

"Without those arms and shoulders of yours, there'd be no Steven, there'd be no Jennifer—I mean it was before my kids were born."

"Well, I couldn't do it today." Wink laughs. He's more cheerful. "Christ, we couldn't do that *climb* today. Some men in their sixties could, but we're out of shape. At least I am."

"No. No. Have another drink," Pete says, and pours.

Wink goes to bed a little drunk, but not too drunk to wake Nan for her midnight pills. Pete, swaying a little, stands by the door as Wink hovers over her bed and murmurs something, and a husky voice fumbles a reply.

Now Pete settles down for the night. Naked in the full-length mirror, he sees himself still lean, but beginning to droop; sees the start of a turkey wattle, sees legs sturdy from tennis but lumpy, full of lumps and bumps, as if a sculptor had patched an old statue to add support. "Well, we *were* grand," he says to himself, "grand as . . . grand." He remembers—sees in his mind's eye sunlight and a boat—an all-day sail to Nantucket a summer the Thompsons visited. The air so clear. Boats and islands delineated precisely. And in this sweet light, that's how he remembers the families: *delineated*, etched against blue sky as if they were ritual dancers miming gestures of certain gods.

Alice Thompson must have been twelve or thirteen that

summer, because she was having her first period. There were whisperings and brooding and deep silences, Nan keeping a wing over her. Pete had always delighted in Alice, and it hurt that she wouldn't soften to him as she usually did. Secrets, secrets. His own daughter, Jennifer, seven that year, was bewildered—she always looked up to Alice. *She still does.* Steven was an infant, and Betsy lay on the deck with Steven at her breast. Nan sat at the prow with Alice, caressing her and singing. Nan's long auburn hair was blowing out of its scarf around her face. Pete remembers her smile.

All this ordinary, astonishing young life going on one afternoon on a twenty-six-foot sailboat, while he and Wink took turns at the helm and the boat leaned against the wind. Now Alice and Jennifer and Steven each have children of their own, days of their own like that day.

Of course, there are the things he chooses not to reimagine about that luminous afternoon. The complexities. He can sense himself stuffing those away in the pouch he always stows somewhere on his person. But never mind. That sail! He takes it to bed with him tonight, remembers, back of his eyes, the light, like a talisman to defend himself against the image of a darkened room, silhouette of a big man hovering over the dim shape of a bed.

Pete wakes to the smell of bacon frying. It's been a long time, fifty points of cholesterol, since he last had bacon for breakfast. He's touched; he knows Wink has done this for his fellow American. He shaves and comes downstairs to coffee and scrambled eggs and bacon, thick-sliced. He remembers the four of them hiking in Cornwall. The eggs every morning—they made you say, *Oh,* this *is what eggs are supposed to be—I never ate eggs before.* So this breakfast feels celebratory, like last night's whiskey. But after, Wink fumbles with the silver, shrugs, starts to speak, just asks, "Want more coffee?"

Always, Pete has thought of Wink as a great bear. Even to the grunts—he grunts when he's trying to say something and having a hard time. Now Wink straightens. "Look here: you don't mind keeping guard a few hours? A meeting I decided to sit in on. Pretty important. When I heard you were coming . . . "

"Of course. Wink. Christ—"

"You can read to Nan. She likes that, especially the poets, poets she knows well, Keats, Whitman, Shakespeare sonnets. It's the music, you know what I mean?"

"Does she understand?"

"God only knows. You get hints and clues, but if she could say, 'Here's what I understand, here's what I remember, here's what I don't,' then she wouldn't have the problem, would she? Sometimes I see her grope for a word. It's hard on her. She gets down, way the hell down, defeated. Imagine Nan defeated? *Nan?*"

Pete can't.

"I'm the fullback, I always have been, Pete. I get the job done, pick up the yardage, but she's the quarterback, she calls the plays. I'll bet you never knew that. I'm not putting myself down—I'm as smart as I need to be, and a lot more worldly-wise than Nan. But she's the one, you know?"

"You love her a lot. Anyone can see."

Wink hunches forward over the table, grunts a couple of times, talks low though there's no need. "I wouldn't say this to a soul but you, Pete. Nan and I—it hasn't been the marriage it looked like. Even when you first met us. Even before Alice. I'll tell you a funny thing. Nan's such a romantic bird—*you* used to call her that, remember?—'bird of bright feathers.' And me—well, you know me. But the funny thing is, *I'm* the closet romantic. I wanted a great romance in my life. And what it *has* been—well, it's been a team, we're teammates. We're partners. It's been Alice, of course. And grandchildren. It's investment portfolios and trust arrangements. It's *getting on*." He grunts low in his chest and fingers the table. "But the past few years—just the past *couple* of years—we've become more—I don't know how to put it—*inter-esting* to one another. So . . . "

"Makes it all the harder."

"Makes it all the harder. Now I'm totally with her, Pete. We've begun to take walks around the room. I pretend it's the Alhambra, or Vence. I point out the sights, and she laughs. Doesn't sound much like me, does it?"

"Does Nan remember Vence? Do you think?"

Wink shrugs his big shoulders.

When Wink leaves, Nan is working with the physiotherapist. Pete thinks about what Wink said last night. *Nobody's been young like us.* So much falsity, he thinks. We were so grand for God's camera. But you got no points from God or whoever was keeping score for acting exactly as you were expected to act and pretending it was a put-on. And their insistence on youth. When they were forty, it wasn't the way the others were forty; when fifty, why, they, they were young, while the others were old and sexless.

And now look: that beautiful woman upstairs. Look.

When Pete began to understand this four or five years ago, he cut his hair short, almost like a monk. He'd always traded on being a handsome man. Well, he stopped. He took long walks and didn't think. Well, he didn't *have* to think, he was weaning himself into retirement. For a while he was almost unbearably sad; hell, *still*—he's still sad. But he felt that for the first time he really inhabited, for better or worse, his life.

He didn't speak about it to Betsy. He didn't speak about it to Wink or Nan. Now he has to simulate the irony he once believed separated them out into a caste of their own. But it's as if he looked at them all, himself included, from the other side of a stroke, other side of the grave—their real beauty, their vanities. Everything seems tainted by vanity.

Still, he knows, there are things he's not ready to give up.

After the therapist goes and before the nurse arrives, he takes tea up to Nan on the same silver tray. He helps her sit up in bed and take her pills with water. They play at being cheerful.

She wears an off-white satin bed jacket. Wink or the therapist must have helped her put it on. Her hair, the auburn it's always been but graying at the roots, is brushed and tied back. The softness of her face surprises him again. With her left hand she lifts her right hand out of her way. He probes her eyes, avoiding notice of the discrepancy between her eyes, between the sides of her face. "So," he starts. "So. We have so much history between us— among the four of us. Now our children carry it on. Steven and Jennifer send their love. They've spoken to Alice. *So* much history."

"Skiing," she says. Just the one word.

"Yes." He pulls his chair closer. "*Skiing.* You do remember?"

As if communication has to travel through great distances to reach her, there's a long silence before she says, "I remember."

"And you remember, oh . . . remember swimming off the rocks near Bandol? We were in our twenties, the three of us, it was before I met Betsy. You remember the afternoon I mean?"

It's too much for her to process. He watches her mouth, drooping clownlike to one side, form but not say words, and he feels ashamed, making her work this hard. He simplifies: "Bandol? *Bandol,* Nan?"

"I remember."

"What do you remember, Nan?"

"I remember . . . " and now sounds spill out, maybe words, and her eyes close in frustration and she takes a breath and says, "everything. I remember *everything.* I even worry . . ."

"What about? You *worry,*" he prompts, as if she might lose the thread.

"At night . . . my sleep . . . I may talk in sleep. . . . Talk things . . . Wink hear. Remember? I remember everything." She sinks back into her pillow.

Now they inhabit the same silence.

"I'm sorry, I had to ask. Forty years, Nan. Dear God. I had to

know. I was scared I was alone in all that remembering. Then it
would be as if it had never happened."

"Remember . . . Vence?"

"Yes. I remember, I remember," Pete says, breathy, almost like
singing the words, but he's uneasy. He wonders, when she remembers "everything," what *everything* does she remember? *He*
sees white sheets, French doors opening on a little balcony, he can
feel Nan's soft body at his fingers and smell the warm, furry scent
of her body after making love. And Nan?

"Remember . . . what?" she asks.

And now he stops, surprised, as if he's found his way into a
strange room. Maybe Nan remembers other things, wants *him* to
remember other things. Maybe *his* is the flawed memory.

And at once, in mind's eye, he sees Nan's look sometime late
that afternoon—if it *was* that afternoon. Was it? A bleak look at
the white wall. All the complexities. Where they'd come to.

"Remember love," he says simply.

And it's enough for her. Still, she's struggling to speak. "You
came to see . . . if I remember? That . . . because . . . why . . . you
came."

"I came to be with you. *And* with Wink. I love Wink." Now he
was sitting at the edge of the bed, stroking her hand on the hurt
side, though she probably couldn't feel it. "But mostly—well, to
*know*. If you didn't remember, it would be like being the last sur-
vivor of a world."

She presses his hand with her good hand. He feels, as he has
always felt, at least these past thirty years, since they both knew
that nothing would ever change in their situation, feels intensely
real in her presence and at the same time feels as if he's playacting,
false not just to Wink and Betsy but to himself. He doesn't fully
understand this feeling. It's grown these past five years. It has to
do with how he's exploited a real love—real, yes, no doubt about
it—for forty years, keeping it in his pocket like a secret piece of

himself, as one in exile might finger a secret seal to remember he was royal. In this way he exploited their love and turned it into theater for an audience of one. This he can't say to Nan, he could never say. In this knowledge he's always been alone.

He strokes her cheeks with his fingertips, wanting her to know he isn't unnerved by her changes. She leans toward him and closes her eyes and he closes his. This is what they have, they have what they have. He doesn't talk about history, she doesn't talk about love.

Wink's home, Wink's up there with Nan. Pete can sometimes think, it's like a strange marriage of the four of them. But of course they don't all know that, so it's not. Often, he wishes he could tell Wink all, or part. Maybe, he thinks, when the eros is really gone. But if that hasn't happened now—if he's still roused by her, soaked in her, not like when they were thirty, rushing to little hotels in back streets in London or New York, but *still, still,* as surely as he was last year at Montreux, when she went "shopping" and he went "fishing" on the lake knowing Wink hated fishing— if not now, when will it happen? And even if it did, he knows he lacks the courage. It's not that he fears Wink would turn away from him—though perhaps he would—but that it would make *Wink* feel the sole inhabitant of a world. What would the guy have left?

*He'd have Nan, you fool. That's what he'd have.* Pete laughs at the grand joke and feels suddenly desolate. At this moment, while upstairs Wink gives her comfort, while maybe they walk around a room that has become a crowded, remembered market in Cairo, while they share something that's grown between them privately all these years, Pete feels as if he's already inhabiting a world of one. As if he's always lived there. Courage—it's not just that he lacks the courage to speak to Wink. It's that he loves holding the secret *secret.* His last vanity. In this endless love affair, maybe he hasn't loved Nan as much as he's loved their *affair.*

From his room, lonely, he calls home. The machine answers—his own voice—though this was the time, late morning in Connecticut, they'd planned to talk. But now Betsy picks up and stops the recording.

Nan's better, Peter reports. And he invents, "She sends her love to you."

"Tell her I want to talk to her as soon as she feels able."

"Of course. Of course. I'll let you know. Not yet, honey."

"How bad is it, Pete? Is it very bad?"

"She's cleaved in two, but with therapy a lot will improve. So Wink says. There's loss of memory, but her memory is coming back to her. I guess she'll be nearly all right."

"And *does* she remember?" Betsy asks.

"She remembers us. She remembers you and me."

"Pete. *No*, Pete. I *mean*," Betsy says, "I'm asking, does she remember *you*? Remember the two of you?"

There's a long transatlantic silence, hiss of the wires. And from within the white noise, Pete can see Betsy sitting in the conservatory they added on last year, the air warm, golden and green. It's late morning; she's wearing her old gardening pants with the many pockets; he imagines her sitting with a cup of coffee and staring at the trays of seedlings she started last week. And for a moment he's there with her, then, trick of the heart, she's there alone; it's like a movie tracking shot, from close-up to long shot, until he's seeing her through glass and the bare branches of March trees in Connecticut. And then there's just this black phone and old furniture and they're thousands of miles apart.

"She remembers."

"Well, that's *good*," Betsy says. "I'm glad. I am glad."

After they say good-bye, as Pete stands at the window staring out at the little railed park, Wink calls through the door, "Pete? Can you come have tea with us? With Nan and me?"

And he collects himself and combs his fingers through his short-cropped hair and goes upstairs to take tea.

# The Builder

So, God is there. Simply *there*. Nothing fancy for Michael, no choral music, no auras or penumbras. No mescaline tricks. Just God. For me—*God*, the word, catches me in the chest and makes my breath pulse, blood thump in my temple—for me it's almost erotic. I feel the danger of the word. But for Michael at that moment, it's ordinary, always there, he just hadn't known how ordinary.

Later, on the drive home past fields flooded with rain and melted snow, foothills of the Berkshires, Michael asks himself, *What was it like?* It was like breath. He breathed in—all right, that was God. He breathed out, and his (impure, exhausted) breath became a part of a perfect God. Odd, it was so simple. It was Saturday morning service, the synagogue suffused with sun through the stained glass of what was once a Congregational church. Being wrapped in the tallith was like being wrapped in God. The knots of the fringes of a prayer shawl symbolize the mitzvot, the commandments for a Jew, but that had nothing to do with what he felt. Rather, it was like being held, held *up*, by hands in a sea.

There was a bat mitzvah in the synagogue that morning. As he'd looked around, he knew that except for the family of the girl and a few others, he was alone. He wanted to call out, "God is here with us now!" Instead, he closed his eyes, trying to ignore the family friends dressed up for the occasion, their eyes wandering, waiting for the service to end so they could get down to the congratulating.

The girl herself was unusually competent in Torah, and she was surrounded by a family of devout Jews he knew slightly. He wondered if they had brought God here. He didn't think so. He said, *Dear One, I know you're also with me in the car, in the woods when I ski, in meetings with clients.* He tried—as I am trying now, dancing on a wire in these words that feel so unfamiliar—not to ask questions, afraid to dislodge the connection, but it's like telling yourself not to think about your breathing. He tried to hold the awareness as he drove home, but it was already gone—

—leaving him not refreshed, open to life, but ragged, tired, brooding, wanting to be alone, away from Jeremy's piano and Karen's worries—*Would there be appetizers enough for the party?* —*There's* something to worry about! He knows it's only Karen's way of expressing stress. But he tightens against her. And heavy in his chest is the work he's supposed to forget on the Sabbath. Not just the ordinary pressures of his business, but Azakarian, George Azakarian, who thickens his lungs, forcing long, turgid breaths.

These days, Michael can't keep things out. He has no skin. Most of the time, I think, we walk around in an extra skin manufactured by some processing plant in Texas or Minnesota. Now, without this skin, he walks through Stop & Shop, and drained by fatigue and contempt, he sees people living in a world not only invented—of *course* invented—but boring, a boring invention, a bad animated cartoon world. Unconvincing. If he could see truly, he could make this supermarket into a sacred space. He can't. The neon, the color on the packages, seem to press upon his sinuses. God's world is blotted out by words and fancy logos. He wants to leave his cart and run. But he needs to bring home appetizers.

Down the next aisle a child howls like an animal. A mother yells, "I already *told* you, *No!* And No means no means no!" over the selling-music.

It's humiliating that after this morning he has so little peace. Look how I am screwing up God's holy instrument—like leaving a violin out in the rain.

As he serves drinks to his friends, he feels he's the only one who has visited, just for a moment, the real world. Four couples: he wants to care about what they say. He's ashamed by his own arrogance. But in the middle of the party, between drinks and dinner, he slips away, sits cross-legged on the floor of his walk-in closet. He says, over and over, *Praise God who has brought the world into Being.* Nothing happens except for stiffness in his hips. Besides, is this how a Jew should act? His place is downstairs. Tell them about Azakarian and the children. Or comfort Stephen, whose mother is dying; Michael remembers what it was like, to lose his mother.

"Michael? *Dinner,* Michael!" He hears Karen's impatience.

At dinner he tells his friends about George Azakarian and the shelter for children: how this nonprofit—Aid for Children in Transition, A.C.T.—found a big Victorian house in a wealthy neighborhood in Springdale for a group home, but the neighbors wouldn't have it. An old story. This, they said, is one of the only decent neighborhoods left in Springdale. "We're talking about a shelter for little kids," Michael told his friends, "children five through twelve. Not disturbed teenagers—little kids taken from families where they're beaten or raped. The neighbors hired a lawyer. Hell, these are the rich and powerful. A.C.T. had the law on its side—could have won a court fight—but these rich bastards would have gotten the legislature to put the squeeze on funding. So, A.C.T. had to back off. And we got called in, Peter and me."

"Tell them why it was you," Karen prompted.

"Because of our work in rehab housing."

"Michael and Peter have a great reputation."

"Anyway, A.C.T.'s going to have to stay where it is. In a semi-slum in Springdale. They want to build an addition. But they haven't got the money. I mean, not even close. And this guy Aza-karian—he wants the impossible."

His friends sympathize, then pass on to other things, but Michael doesn't follow them. He remembers Azakarian's pho-tographs: two smiling children, one seven, one four. Next, the little one lying crumpled like a rag, a police photo. *His brother lives with us now; his mother is wasted on drugs, his stepfather is awaiting trial.* Michael picks at his roast and for comfort rocks slightly, like an old Jew in synagogue, not so anyone can see.

But Karen has seen. And later—"Do you think it's a pleasure to live with you in these moods?"

"It's not something I want to talk about. Something good happened. In synagogue today—"

"*Today!* Michael, you've been this way for months. Maybe a year. You're getting so peculiar. Michael, look at you, look in the mirror. 'Something good'?—It's like you're in mourning. For whom? Who died?"

He could tell her, but he doesn't; he takes his pillow and once again sleeps wrapped in self-righteousness in the study.

Monday morning begins with the usual planning meeting, Mi-chael Kahn and Peter Malley. They've got an architectural design firm just outside Green River. House Smiths is more than a design firm; it's a company that designs and builds houses—they prefab a lot of the components themselves in a big steel building they were able to pick up for a song in 1990 when businesses were dropping like flies; they rode out the recession and now they're squeezed for space.

Michael's the front man, he shmoozes with architects and clients. I conjure him to be good-looking, lean; thick hair still black; he has tender eyes that really look at you and a kind smile, though he hasn't been smiling lately. Peter, powerful, balding, he's the money man, positioning the business for sale in a few years so they can both retire, if they feel inclined, just past fifty—not bad for a couple of leftist carpenters, hippie carpenters, who met on a commune in Vermont, early seventies. Peter's father was an inventor, a tinkerer, a genius with tools. Peter built his own dresser, with his father's help, at age seven. But Michael grew up in Boston, son of a research psychologist father and a sociologist mother, and hardly used a hammer until he needed a summer job in college. For him, doing carpentry was partly carrying on the quarrel with his father.

As was being a Jew.

For to be a practicing Jew was to slip back out of the modern world, to be like his grandfather, his father's father. His mother wouldn't have minded—she was tender with the old man. His father would have rolled his eyes.

His grandfather lived in the third-floor apartment they fixed up in the big Edwardian house in Brookline, Mass. Michael's mother used to walk him to shul. Later, when Michael was eight, nine, ten, he was the one who walked with his grandfather Saturday mornings, and the old man would hum synagogue melodies in anticipation. That was Michael's Jewish education. If his grandfather had lived a little longer, Michael might have been bar mitzvahed. After his grandfather's death, when Michael had time to himself, he would climb the servant stairway to the third floor and knock. "Grandpa? *Zeide?*" It was a word between the two of them, *Zeide*, for when he forgot and called his grandfather *Zeide* at dinner, his father would lift his eyebrows, and Michael would correct himself—"Grandpa."

There was a different smell to the third floor. Old-man smell, smoked fish on his breath, dusty upholstery of cast-off furniture, gaberdine that never went to the cleaners. Michael liked to breathe in the smell, though it was sour, strange, and half of what his grandfather talked about he didn't understand. I mean, not at all. Yiddish, Hebrew. Stories about the long dead. Later, when he was a teenager and his *zeide* was dead, he'd sometimes take a book up to the third floor, by then shut up, dim, storerooms really, and sit on the sagging red velvet sofa to read.

"Your grandfather is from another century," his father would say. "He still lives in Odessa." And Michael believed this. His father played his collection of jazz records and felt they somehow made him part of modern America. Upstairs, Jacob Kahn sang in Yiddish or chanted in Hebrew; he had a quavering but rich voice, and it wasn't until Michael was seven or eight that he stopped acting as part-time cantor. So then it was only Michael who listened. When his father overheard, he would roll his eyes. He permitted the old man to say a blessing at table, while he, Ira, busied himself salting his food.

So now, being a practicing Jew has been like undergoing conversion. He inherited his grandfather's prayer shawl, and now, when he wraps himself in the shawl, he imagines his grandfather within his flesh.

My own grandfather, also Jacob, was dead before I was born. I wish he'd lived upstairs. He's the old man whose photos hang on the wall of my study, heavy beard and the wide-brimmed black hat and long black coat, grandfather with my grandmother and seven children, two almost grown, my mother the youngest, a studio portrait taken just after they arrived in America, 1906, after the pogrom in Kishnief.

Why do I need this other grandfather and this "Michael" between us—between you and me? Michael is a word fumbling toward becoming a person. That's always true of a character in

a story. But *Michael himself* feels like a character. Before anyone else was awake this morning, he looked in the mirror and
was unfamiliar to himself. He didn't dislike the man he saw,
but who was it, anyway? The only person with whom he felt at
home was the one aware of the incongruity, asking questions
with his eyes.

I know what that's like. Sometimes I read one of my old
stories and wonder who wrote it. Michael feels like the author of
his life; but that means his life is . . . just a story—and in a sense,
not even *his*. For several seconds this morning he stood outside
the company entrance trying to inhabit the body of the lean,
middle-aged man in clean jeans and expensive Shetland wool
sweater so he could walk into the building without feeling like an
imposter. He didn't mind borrowing this particular person to
live in; he had nothing against him. But it was a borrowing.

This Monday morning, he and Peter go through current projects
and prospects, pull in their three project managers for briefings,
cope with schedules, problems, ruffled feelings. It's spring, peak
season for them. Peter—recently remarried—groans, his way of
bragging, that he's recovering from an all-day Sunday love ses-
sion. Michael pats his shoulder and grins as he's meant to. They
*don't* talk about the group home. Alone in his office, whine of the
mill, factory noises, mostly insulated out, he puts the yarmulke
on his head, wraps himself in his grandfather's tallith, and says
the morning Shema.

On his walls are pictures of completed buildings—a cohousing development he's particularly proud of, a whole street of rehab apartments, the rest subdivision houses, modular but each
unique and strong. He likes what this "Michael" does. But from
the quiet of his prayers he sees Michael's life a complicated fabrication, substantial and invented as architecture. He feels he
might tiptoe out of Michael's body and let it go on doing. Then he
could slip out of the invented world into the world God made.

God isn't here this morning, not like in synagogue the other day. But the world out the window, the parking lot, the orchard across the road, the hillside beginning to green, hum with living silence.

Peter raps and enters, already talking about a bid he's preparing for Smith College, and Michael has to reenter the invented world. He folds the prayer shawl away, feels like a high school kid caught with a cigarette. Peter squints, taps the crown of his own head. "That thing, what d'you call it?"

"This? A yarmulke." Michael covers it with his palm as if protecting.

"Yeah. So. You gonna wear that 'yamuka' with clients around?"

Michael pulls out a file and ignores him. Peter opens his arms and raises his palms, accepting the burden of this craziness. "Hey. It's okay with me you get a little nuts." But he doesn't leave.

"*What?*"

"You're *not* gonna wear that . . . *shawl* thing?"

"Not with clients. It's for prayer."

"Well Ah'm fuckin' relieved."

Michael hears Peter pretending to be crude, playing the role of tough ignoramus as a way of putting himself into a comic posture, and Michael, aware of the subtle delicacy, the kindness under the toughness, smiles at him tenderly.

Peter squinches up his face, refusing the generous eyes. He hates bullshit and looks it. He's a thick man, built like a wrestler—*a Sumo wrestler,* he jokes sometimes, rubbing his balding head and thrusting out his belly, pouting his lips. "I realize we didn't talk about the group home. Later, okay? Now *there's* a can of worms."

Michael gets on the phone to clients. He drives out to oversee the million-dollar showplace he's building for Mr. Gianapoulos in the hills above the Connecticut Valley. The land is being cleared. Gianapoulos is poking around today, so Michael has to stand with him admiring the view, as if Gianapoulos had made the valley he sweeps with his hand.

When he gets back, George Azakarian is waiting for him. A bloated man in his forties, man with a thick nose and thinning hair, Azakarian has apparently just finished a bag lunch in the waiting room; there are crumbs on the rug, stains and cigarette ash on the shapeless sports jacket he always wears and on his tie. Azakarian may be the last man on earth, surely in the Connecticut Valley, to wear a bow tie. Which he ties himself. Badly. His shirt is missing a button; it's a cotton shirt that needs ironing. All this is disarming. You feel comfortable with the slob, and then he puts the squeeze on.

Azakarian brushes himself off and follows Michael into his office. He smells of cigarette smoke. "I don't mean to badger you," he says, "but what's this message you left on my machine? I don't understand, Mr. Kahn. *Michael.* I thought we had an arrangement, Michael. I've put a lot of time into this."

"Sit down. Please. Look—you guys are a hundred thousand underbudgeted. A lot of the problem is disability access, sprinklers, all that crap. It's state requirements, I know, but whoever you work with, nobody can do it for the price you're talking."

"With you. We're working with you."

Michael closes his eyes.

"There are six children in the house; too many as it is. And we need space for twelve more. The good people of Springdale decided that their property values—"

"I know, I know that. It was in the papers. My partner—"

"I'm not dealing with your partner."

"Every agency guilt-trips the builder, Mr. Azakarian. Every time we do a rehab or cohousing, they want a benefit performance. Tell me—do you take a cut in your salary?"

Azakarian laughs. "*My* salary?"

"Okay. I get it. But look: this is our *business.* We wouldn't be here if we didn't make a profit."

"Did I ask you for charity?"

"Essentially—yes."

"You remember the photographs I showed you? I ask you to think hard about those children," Azakarian says on his way out. And as if in afterthought: "You have children, Mr. Kahn?"

Michael asks back: "Do *you?*"

"All told, resident and nonresident, forty-three of them, Mr. Kahn."


Their usual cost-plus contract gives them a ten percent edge. "Suppose we drop my part of the profit," he says to Peter. "Cut it to five percent."

"It's not just profit, Michael, it's money for the business."

"You can take it out of my bonus the end of the year."

"Oh for chrissakes. Don't fuckin' insult me. Sometimes you can get so goddamn smug," Peter says. He sits on Michael's desk. "You really think it's the five percent? Don't insult me. It's spreading ourselves too thin. We take on this, we can't concentrate on that—and *that,* m'man, is work for Smith College. *Money.* Eight hundred thousand. You take on a little project for A.C.T., it'll eat up the same effort. Am I wrong?"

"You're not wrong. And as it is, they don't have the money."

"We're not a charity."

"We're not. That's what I told him."

"Tell him you'll cut him a check, give them a couple hundred. Okay?"


For a while he can keep the two of him going at once. God is not at his beck and call; but there are times. There get to be times in an ordinary day when he has to stop the car on the way home because everything he sees is suffused with the same single life, the same being, and it's not a world of *things;* or it is and it isn't, for there are certainly "things," but they are all conjoined. Praise God who has brought the world into Being. This is Being.

And so he tells Mr. Gianopoulos, for whom he's building a 1.2-million-dollar house on that beautiful piece of land overlooking the valley, Mr. Gianopoulos, who's a haggler, a cranky, pompous son of a bitch who owns a trio of gas stations, that if the house they're building for him were turned thirty degrees, oriented so that the morning light could enter *there*, it would invite God in. "This way, you see?" Michael says pointing to the screen, turning the computer model in relation to a computer sun, "God will be there. Well," he laughs, "God is always there, but this way you'd feel it, you'd feel it. Every morning—imagine!—you'll feel God's light like breath through your house."

They don't lose the account, but Peter has to take it over. "I'm sorry," Michael says. "I got carried away."

"Suppose Gianopoulos doesn't believe in God."

"Belief is beside the point, Pete. I'm not interested in a God you 'believe' in—or don't 'believe' in. Belief's got nothing to do with it."

"Well, hear me—I'm not interested in what you fuckin' *feel*, if we're talking feeling. Okay?"

This time, no kind comic posture.

Azakarian stops by just as Michael is to leave for the day. He stands and brushes himself off; always he's got something *to* brush off, in this case, crumbs from tortilla chips. "Don't think I want to badger you—"

"Of course you want to badger me."

"Look, Mr. Kahn: the situations we face are getting worse and worse. We talk about making transitions for children to go back to their families. But there *are* no families. The children have always had multiple problems, but the problems have gotten worse, and money is being cut back. We've run out of possibilities, Michael." He opens his hands to show there's nothing up his sleeve.

"So that's my responsibility?"

"You ought to come for a visit."

Michael drives from Green River down to Springdale. Springdale is a defeated mill city, maybe sixty percent on public assistance. He's got work to do—supervising the rehabing of new apartments in six adjoining tenement buildings in the poorest section of town.

As he drives, he chants the Amidah.

He irritates me, this Michael. It's not hard to love God-in-the-world through the window of a Volvo as you pass cows pastured under a hillside. What about in Springdale?

In Springdale, he passes boarded-up stores, whole streets the city has taken in default of taxes, covering the windows with plywood so that the buildings look like frightening dead things. Can he tell those two overweight young women pushing babies in strollers that there is available to them a world in which God is present? The children will go to a fire-trap school—he's been there to consult on renovations—where the money goes for boiler repairs and heat that escapes through cracks in the old brick, cracks you can see through, and the teachers have thirty-five kids, including kids with special problems, some with hardly any English, instead of the fifteen in Jeremy's class. In a world this crippled, what does it mean to bless? To put it plainly—does the blessing make him an accomplice in the crippling? Michael tells himself, *Oh, but this crippled world, that's not God's world; it's the world people invented, it's Babylon—where the poor are, with a shrug, shoved out of sight into their poverty.* And isn't he doing something to unmake Babylon?

He and Peter make a very good guaranteed profit on rehab housing.

On his way to the job, he drives a few blocks out of his way to see an A.C.T. home. A.C.T. runs a facility in an old two-family house on a dead-end street. It's nothing fancy, but it's clean. The kids seem okay. Three running around or climbing, one standing, rocking himself against a chain-link fence. They're dressed warm, there's a woman watching out for them. He looks into a window. Drab but not filthy. Still, he thinks about Jeremy living in a place this bleak. Out of sight of the kids, he prays to try to get sadness out of his chest. He doesn't go inside.

It's Friday evening; he tries to find refuge in the Sabbath. He has to shop again; home, he unloads his bags and his heart, sits down with Karen and Jeremy to light the Shabbat candles and say the prayers. Karen goes along with this for his sake. Jeremy likes the ritual; he's the one to light the candles as Michael says the prayers in Hebrew and English. In the silence afterward, Michael finds his hands, eyes, mouth, lungs, opening; everything will work out. The children, this marriage, our common life. He is so open he has to catch his breath. "God," he announces, "is here. Now. Is here with us tonight."

Karen scrunches up her eyes. He knows that tilt of her head to one side: she doesn't know how to take him. She reaches under the table to take hold of Jeremy's hand. Michael understands the gesture as part of an ongoing dialogue from which he's been excluded.

He reassures her. "The world that God has created: look: it's simple: it's here, *we're* here *in* it." He opens his hands as if catching rain, and combs his finger through the charged air.

"I'm glad for you," she says. She doesn't look glad. "Michael? Are you here at the table, Michael? We're having dinner, all right? Look. I made coq au vin instead of roast chicken. And I bought a challah for you."

Jeremy seems to understand that his father is not speaking in metaphor. He won't let go with his eyes. Michael wants to reassure. But what can he say? *I love coq au vin?*

God no longer seems to be with them.

To write about a man experiencing the world-God-made, the world of Being, it's as if I am wearing a fish-smelling beard in western Massachusetts. Michael becomes a fool; these words make me a fool. They don't work anymore. I'm supposed to speak the language of the invented world. But it's so clumsy for expressing the world of Being. How do I talk about the world that God makes and makes and continues making? Michael invites God into the world; I invite God into a "realistic" story. The form is strained; it wants to see Michael as "disturbed."

Well, and isn't he disturbed? God knows he is. God-crazed, his eyes inappropriate for overseeing construction, he walks out on a scaffolding over a two-story living room in his father's old fedora coated in sheetrock dust and pretends not to notice the carpenters grin at one another. Even at synagogue he feels that people are looking at him curiously. He makes an appointment to speak to the rabbi.

Rabbi Singer is in his early thirties. Michael likes him but wishes he were at least seventy, with thick breath and deep-set eyes. He doesn't tell him God appeared to him in synagogue. He says, "I can't walk through the mall without tears coming to my eyes. I can't look at the *New York Times*."

"Well, the *newspaper,* of course, of course."

"There's a story about Tutsi women raped by Hutus, and now the women are outcast, the women and their children, and terrorized as well. Or I read about the great famine in China in the early sixties—as many as thirty million died. That's five Holocausts."

"There's no comparison—" the rabbi begins.

"That's not my point, Rabbi. It's that on the next page there are recipes for peppering foods, there are sexy men and women in jeans. Furs are 'in.' There's fabulous new architecture in New Zealand. This is nothing new, I understand. An old story, Rabbi."

"Of course. Terrible ironies. Cognitive dissonance."

"It's dissonance—but not 'cognitive.' I sit at the kitchen table and weep. And then there's God's world, it's here and we can't live in it. It's dissonance of the heart, and how do you live with that?"

The rabbi nods his head. "I think you're seeing accurately, Mr. Kahn, you're certainly seeing what's there. But the *weeping . . .* " Haltingly, he suggests that Michael "seek help." He means not divine guidance but a psychotherapist.

At night he is afraid to go to sleep, because lately dreams have been engulfing him like a deadly sea; in the morning he feels exhausted by the struggle. People turn to God to give them stability. Michael *used* to be stable; God has destablized him.

As he dresses, mornings, he becomes aware that he has been inhabited by his grandfather. It slows down his walk. Odessa has come to western Massachusetts. Michael remembers when he was a little boy and his grandfather went around their house humming synagogue melodies, murmuring the Hebrew with its heavy *ch* sounds that relieve the heart. His breathing was so labored that sometimes Michael was afraid to stand near someone whose bronchia were constantly singing of death. Yet now, he can't do without him.

Inhabiting his grandfather, he is astonished by the microwave, the VCR, the pastures and hills appearing and disappearing with magic speed as Michael drives to work. To make his grandfather feel at home, he stops shaving. It isn't a decision exactly; one day he forgets to shave, and Karen goes off for a weekend workshop, so he doesn't have to shave, and when she comes back he has the beginning of a beard. He has a picture of his *zeide* in a photographer's studio. The old man is trying to be American; in this picture he is not wearing his black hat. Michael, brought up American, needs to become a greenhorn.

So he stops shaving, he grows his sideburns and twists the ends into the beginnings of earlocks. He doesn't wear a skullcap but the old fedora. A fedora doesn't go with a zip-up windbreaker. It's as if he has to re-create his grandfather's condition, make himself a mourner and a pariah—he is making himself a pariah fast—in order to have the privilege of loving God as his grandfather did.

Karen says, "If I wanted to marry your marvelous grandfather, I'd have gone to the lubvavitcher in Brooklyn."

Peter takes him to lunch and talks about buying him out.

For school vacation, Karen takes Jeremy to her parents—just half an hour away. "At a time like this, I don't want to leave you alone, Michael—no, really, I don't—but I worry what this is doing to Jeremy. The way you look. And it's not just the way you look. It's all right that you pray, but I catch you standing at the window and rocking, davening. This isn't a synagogue. Michael? Even the way you *breathe*, so heavy . . . "

"I can shave. You want me to shave?" And when she doesn't answer, he asks, "Are you coming back?"

Karen shrugs. "It's not been so great lately, Michael."

Michael sits with Jeremy in his bedroom the night before they leave. He puts his arm around him and feels him stiffen. "It's all right, honey. I've got a beard, but I'm not crazy."

Suddenly, Jeremy hugs him back, furiously.

Alone, he eats tuna out of cans, doesn't change his underwear. He prays, he's a prayer junkie, waking early to pray, getting to work late, sneaking prayers at his desk, not taking home bids to work over but reading Torah. The required three times a day he prays, and then he stops the car and walks in the woods to talk to God. Prayers that always seemed empty, circular—*Praise God, who is to be praised* (vainglorious, as if God were a sports hero, as if this were a celebrity God who needed praise, basked in it)—now, at the good times, they seem so clear: instructions to attune yourself, like adjusting the dial, to what hums beneath things, divesting yourself of glories customarily praised: the meretricious. False gods. It doesn't matter if I can retire at fifty with an income. It doesn't matter if Karen wins High School Teacher of the Year. All he wants is to live in the part of himself that's holy because it's permeated with God.

As I, too, want to enter the original world. These words, a prayer. I use words to get beyond words, hammer and nail this strange space. But then I'm shut off inside the words I make. I hardly know what it's like outside—I mean this earth, the sun, squirrels trekking across my deck rail. I sit typing these words and forget what's outside the window and the people who can't say where their next meal is coming from or how to pay the doctor. The words are a clumsy prayer, but the words keep me outside the only world God can find to inhabit. It's an occupational hazard.

After the week's vacation, Karen begins to commute to school—temporarily, she says—from her parents' house instead of returning home. Michael broods about Jeremy and is reminded of the Akeda—Abraham's willingness to sacrifice Isaac before God's release of them both. Yes, God's release—but think of the trauma, *the walk home, father and son!* Is he, Michael, sacrificing Jeremy? He thinks about the children at Azakarian's shelter. He's made Jeremy one step closer to their condition. To be in God's world, does that make him complicitous in injury, like Abraham?

He wants his family back. He knows he needs to stop this.

He asks Peter to meet him in the conference room. He can see himself in Peter's eyes. "So I look that bad?"

"That old dirty hat on your head, your dirty beard—they think you're crazy, the guys. D'you know that? *Are* you crazy? You want to take a crazy leave?"

And Michael doesn't argue. It's like he's *using* Pete's anger the way the *penitente* used whips to scourge themselves.

"We've got something going here, you fuck it up you're doing it to both of us. Man, you've got to pull your weight. I'd sue your ass, I'd find a clause, but we're supposed to be friends." He turns away.

"Peter? I'm thinking maybe I should build for Azakarian. For A.C.T. A home for the children."

Peter sighs. Michael can see his friend and partner leafing mentally through the company's medical insurance policy. "I thought we decided we're not a charity, Mike."

"I'm not talking charity. I want . . . to make a home for God."

This is too much. Peter picks up his sheaf of papers.

"'Let them make me a sanctuary that I may dwell among them.' God says that in Exodus. The passage is talking about a tabernacle, but why limit it? Please. A month, a couple of months. But only part-time, Pete. Pete, I'll keep on with other projects. And look—I'll pay us back, hour for hour."

"You can't separate it out like that. You're needed full-time. And the thing is, it's not *you* that's needed. It's the guy you've always been." He's quiet for a minute, pokes at his papers. "I need him," he says quietly.

"*Call* it crazy leave, if you want."

"Oh, Michael. We've been together twenty years. What the fuck." Peter turns and puts his two big hands on Michael's hairy cheeks. "Please be okay."

Azakarian's phone rings and rings; no message machine picks up. He wants to settle this tonight before he changes his mind, so he drives down to Green River to drop off a note. Azakarian lives in one part of a small two-family house on a street of two-family houses. A street of workers' houses from a time when Green River was a booming industrial town. It's drizzling. Under the street lamp, one side of the lawn is cluttered with toys—a plastic car, a soccer ball, a refrigerator carton with windows and doors cut out of the wet cardboard. On Azakarian's side, nothing.

Michael stands on the sagging porch and tries to see inside.

Lights upstairs give him a dim view. The living room is pure Azakarian—shabby, papers piled everywhere, a vinyl couch that looks like it was borrowed from a dying motel. No, Azakarian's not married. He hears voices, music, faint, tinny, from upstairs: a TV. So he rings.

No answer . . . no answer—he's about to put the note into the mailbox next to the buzzer when the stairwell light comes on, the television gets louder. Heavy thump of Azakarian on the stairs.

For a few seconds, Azakarian doesn't seem to know him. Michael is instantly sorry he came. Beer on his breath. He's been sleeping or drunk; his hair, what there is of it, has come down in all directions. Sure, drunk. He's wearing no belt, the top button of his pants is undone.

"Is this a bad time?"

"No, no. It's okay."

"We can talk tomorrow," Michael says. But he comes in.

The bitter smell of old cigarette smoke mixed with dried sweat from unwashed clothes; that, he expected. The sour smell of beer is a surprise, the books are a surprise. What looked like papers through the window turn out to be books and magazines spilled out onto the floor, onto the couch, onto the varnished spool for electric line that serves as coffee table. He can't find a place to sit.

"All these books . . . "

"It's my hobby. I read history. Let me get you a drink. Here . . . " Azakarian clears the sofa with a sweep of his arm and goes upstairs to turn off the TV. Michael tilts his head to look at the titles. History? No history he could see. Detective fiction, soft porn magazines. Azakarian comes back with two cans of beer, two dirty glasses. "I unplug the phone at night when I'm not on call." Now he stops, scrunches up his eyes, bleary eyes. "What's happened to you? Since I saw you last? A beard, of course. You grew yourself a beard. What's the matter? You sick?"

Michael feels the comedy of this. A couple of ragged guys

each seeing the other as ragged and peculiar. He doesn't want to talk about it, it gets to him. But then he laughs at the two of them. If, in his half-stupor, Azakarian's shocked, I must really look like something! He takes off his fedora and leans forward. "All right. Forget what I look like. Here's what I'm willing to do." He stops. "Tell me. Are you okay enough to understand what I'm saying?"

"*Sure.* Sure. Just a couple of beers."

"I'll organize the construction for you. On my own. Weekends, evenings. I'll do the hiring, I'll handle the project, and I'll charge nothing except what I have to lay out for labor and materials."

"That's reasonable."

"Reasonable!" He laughs but lets it slide. "Even so, it'll come in over budget—but . . . maybe we can handle it. Now, Mr. Azakarian, will you work with me? Because listen—you keep trying to guilt-trip me, you ask for more and more, and I'll walk away."

"Of course, of course."

*Of course, of course,* but inside his belly Michael feels a moan wanting to float up: it's Azakarian's mess rising up in him. It's as if he could feel Azakarian's life from inside; the attempt makes him thick, blurred. "The house in Springdale looks pretty nice—"

"—Good! You went to look."

"—But *you*—you don't look so good. I worry when I look at you. Let me tell you plainly, I worry. Can you handle it?"

Azakarian doesn't answer. He walks around the room collecting beer cans, straightening books, clearing a leather chair with a gash in the seat. "Daytimes, I can."

"I see."

Azakarian says, "So we better talk in the daytime." He grunts. "Tomorrow. Tomorrow I won't look like this. . . . You let yourself out." And he climbs the stairs, not looking back.

"I'm sorry," Michael calls after him. "Hey. Don't *worry.*"

"You don't look so good yourself, you know."

A door shuts. Michael is left in this room strewn with papers. He prowls. The kitchen sink is as he expects. The fridge is full of moldy food, the freezer compartment thick with nothing but frost—you couldn't squeeze in a box of frozen peas. Underneath the vegetable bin is a pool of water growing mold. How can this damaged man provide a home for damaged children?

He should go home, he should sleep, but he sits and sits, squashed by the chaos.

So he begins by finding a pail and a utility sponge in the kitchen closet. At first the idea is to suggest to Azakarian that he should clean up his act. But that idea dissolves within the first few minutes, and he doesn't know why, but he's getting rid of the pool of scum at the bottom of the fridge, the old containers of mold or dried-up soup that had separated from the plastic. It starts with the scum, but then he realizes he has to defrost or the freezing compartment will drip a new pool. So he boils two big pots of water, and while he cleans the kitchen, he lets one pot sit in the freezing compartment, then the other, until he can pop the solid ice with a screwdriver and sponge the mess into a pail. And then it's the racks, so he can get to the mildew on the ceramic walls, until the fridge is immaculate and bare except for a container of milk and a six-pack.

That feels good—until he notices the mildew on the walls, finds Clorox and detergent and goes to work, while the dishwasher cleans the dishes.

He still has energy. Energy or anxiety; he can't sleep, what the hell, so he turns to the living room. He thinks of stories of fairy godmothers and giggles, imagining Azakarian waking up. But nothing, not even dumping cans in a green garbage bag, wakes Azakarian. The magazines—none of his business—he piles in a corner, the books on the coffee table. He straightens the chairs and pulls the diagonal bump out of the rug.

He listens. Okay. Even if he *vacuums*, Azakarian will sleep! Michael goes to work with an old Electrolux, feeling pleasure when bits of dried cracker and chips, sand carried in from the winter, ancient nuts and raisins ting, ting up the nozzle. Until the living room rug is without obvious dirt—though now the stains show up even worse.

It clears his own head. Stopping, he combs the air with open fingers, inviting God in.

It's after one in the morning when he finally slips out, drives home, and even then not to sleep right away. He sits down at his desk to make lists of jobs. He goes through the names of members of the synagogue and culls out the lawyers, the owner of a building supply company, a banker. Then there is his own money. He's got savings for retirement, for Jeremy's college. He doesn't touch his IRAs but makes a note to himself to withdraw twenty thousand from his cash reserves and open a special account. Not something to tell Azakarian, but it'll be there.

Before going to bed, he looks at himself in the bathroom mirror—Be honest—can he *schnorr* money with a beard like this? Regretfully, as he's known he must, he shaves; regretfully, he throws the fedora in the garbage. Well, by now it's gray with sawdust and stained with machine oil. He slicks down his hair. Like a zoo creature, he wanders the empty house, every few minutes stopping to look at his face in a mirror. He doesn't feel close to this person; a competent professional. Clean-cut and feeling efficient again, he finds it harder to pray tonight. He says the Shema, but the words seem to go nowhere. And tomorrow—a haircut.

Karen and Jeremy are home again, Karen a little too solicitous. Oh, it's *Peter,* Michael is sure—Peter, worried, must have got on the phone to her. She's relieved to see him looking normal. *Looking yourself,* she says. They're polite to one another, kind, even, as they cut up vegetables and put out plates. They're not lovers yet, but at night she holds his hand and once takes his head to her breast.

Peter is equally relieved, and, to show it, has become conspicuously generous to the project, pulling off workers from other jobs, offering free use of forms for pouring the foundation, costing out parts of the job because he's better at it than Michael.

It's a Saturday morning, more than a month after the cleaning of Azakarian's. He's never been back there, and Azakarian never spoke about it, but there's less bullshit between them now, less "Have you considered the children, Mr. Kahn?" Sometimes Azakarian stops by to go over plans. Once they went out for coffee and talked about finishing materials. Azakarian's okay during the day, and Michael doesn't ask about nights. It's a tough job, human services, what the hell.

The foundation's done, exterior walls are framed and sheathed. On this Saturday morning Jeremy wanted to see the work, maybe help, or just be with his father, so Michael drives down with him to Springdale. He's there instead of synagogue because on Monday the electricians are coming to rough in the wiring, and he needs to make sure they'll be ready. But once he's there, he goes to work. One guy's framing interior walls, one putting up sheetrock. A table saw whines. He shows Jeremy how to nail up sheetrock, and he takes over the cutting, getting the pieces ready for Jeremy.

It's like praying with his hands, he thinks. It's okay to be here on the Sabbath. He wants, fervently, to believe this, to believe that he's helping to rebuild God's world. His hands and clothes are filled, as in the old days, with sawdust. God's world smells of machine oil and sawdust.

Still, he misses something, and there's no one he can tell. He misses the Original World. It's God's presence he misses, it's God he feels he's had to say good-bye to: like saying good-bye to a lover at a rendezvous and having to face the dreariness of all the rest of your life without her.

He takes charge of the framing. The ring of the nail gun

thrums through his chest. Country music from a boom box keeps the work moving. He wants to feel himself part of a congregation. As he cuts wood or slams in nails, he tries to imagine that he is building a world for God to inhabit.

It's a warm day; kids are out back on the playground's climbing structure. Two boys want to be in on it; they stand in the doorway looking cool. "It's okay with me," Michael says, "if you help Jeremy with the sheetrock. It needs to be held in place." One, a boy about Jeremy's age, gets into it.

The work takes on a rhythm, it's like a dance, the three men, Jeremy, and this boy. And both the work and these words with which I shape the work, shape Michael's sad peace this morning—both become a prayer, the same prayer in two languages.